Coll 2

The Turning Tide

and other stories

Gervase Phinn

with best wishes,

Gervase Phinn

Nelson

Thomas Nelson and Sons Ltd
Nelson House Mayfield Road
Walton-on-Thames Surrey
KT12 5PL UK

Thomas Nelson Australia
102 Dodds Street
South Melbourne
Victoria 3205 Australia

Nelson Canada
1120 Birchmount Road
Scarborough Ontario
M1K 5G4 Canada

© **Gervase Phinn**
First published by Thomas Nelson and Sons Ltd 1990

I(T)P Thomas Nelson is an International
Thomson Publishing Company

I(T)P is used under licence

ISBN 0-17-439216-8
NPN 9 8 7 6 5 4 3 2

Cover illustration: Phil Bannister
Illustrations: Peter Bailey, Judy Brown, Sian Davies, Pauline King, Kaoru Miyake,
Tony Morris, Martin Salisbury and Carol Wright.
Printed in China

Contents

Introduction

For as long as there have been people gathered around the fire telling and re-telling tales of adventure and magic, there have been short stories: varied in subjects and ideas and situations.

The eleven short stories in this collection reflect this diversity. There are sad, strange, humorous, tender and supernatural stories, varied in length, theme, style and mood. The one thing they have in common is that they all deal with aspects of life confronting young people: growing up in a particular environment; attitudes to parents and friends, to teachers and the elderly; the successes, tensions and disappointments of school; relationships with brothers and sisters - a whole variety of subjects and situations about which pupils will have opinions.

The follow-on activities at the end of the anthology offer ideas for discussion, for writing and for further reading, encouraging pupils to respond to the stories in a wide variety of ways.

A Present from the Hartz Mountains

by Gene Kemp

The trouble is nobody believes me. Not that I blame them really. That bump on the head, they say, that's what did it. Tripping over the root of a tree. But I didn't trip. I was pushed, I said when I got back home

'Who by? No one was near you at the time,' said my sister Jill, stuffing down pizza like one of the starving. I couldn't eat mine.

'I'll give you an aspirin and you can lie down for a bit,' said my Mum, who's really a step-mum, but not a wicked one, she says.

'I don't want to lie down. I'm not ill.'

'You don't look all right.'

'He looks round the twist. Bonkers. Barmy. That's because he is,' said Jill, eating a slice of cake.

I didn't like that. I was afraid I might be. David Clarke, nutcase, me.

'You'll be all right tomorrow,' said my mum.

'I'm all right now.'

Jill pulled faces and tapped her forehead. This was hopeless. I might as well go to bed. I turned round in the doorway.

'But what about the witch?' I shouted.

'What about the witch?' shrugged Jill and twisted up her nose at me.

The witch had arrived that morning, in the post for Jill with a box of sweets for me, fantastic sweets in weird shapes and colours, like nothing I've ever seen before.

Presents from the Hartz Mountains, West Germany, the label read.

'It's from your Aunt Kate. She's on holiday there,' said Mum.

She'd also sent a postcard covered with fir trees.

'Having a super holiday in Grimm country. Very mysterious forest. You'd like it. All the best witches live here. I'm sending one for you. Don't be good. Luv, Aunt Kate.'

A flyaway witch on a tiny wooden broomstick, with a hooked, green nose, red shiny eyes, gruesome grey hair, a black hat and a tatty black cloak. I didn't like it one little bit.

'Witches are rubbish,' I said.

'I'm taking her on the school trip,' Jill announced.

'Do you have to? You're bound to lose it,' protested Mum.

'If she's taking that object, then I'm taking my sweets to eat with my packed lunch. And she's not having any.'

'It's your gracious charm that makes life with you two so worthwhile,' said Mum, handing us our orange juice, our lunches and spending money. But Jill and my mate Jonathan ate the sweets, as I didn't fancy them much, and Mo, Jill's friend, who'd tagged along with us, said 'They're beautiful, but no-one in their right mind would eat sweets like that, not all those colours and shapes'. Funny she should say that for Mo can't possibly be all there, or how come she puts up with Big Bossy Boots Jill all the time?

'We're coming with you to eat our packed lunch,' she said to Jonathan and me. 'Me and Mo are coming with you.'

We'd managed to keep out of her way all morning, mainly because she's third year and we're fourth year but in the end she'd caught up with us.

'Oh, all right, then.'

The teachers said we could eat where we liked but we were to meet up again at the monkey house at two to be checked and counted.

'Don't get us muddled with the monkeys, will you, Sir?' Jonathan grinned. He's a joker. He's also big and black and the best footballer in the school so when Gary Ronchetti muttered 'That's only likely to happen in your case', he just stared at him and Gary backed away, saying 'I didn't mean that, honest, you know I didn't'.

Not that I cared. Jonathan could fight his own battles.

My head ached for the air bounced and shimmered with heat and the Wild Life Park we were visiting seemed like a jungle, full of shouts and noise and peacocks shrieking.

'Watch out for poisonous snakes,' shouted Jill, shooting

up behind us. 'They say the undergrowth's full of them.'

That was all I needed, snakes.

Plus the dozen other schools all on their school trips, the blazing blue sky and the animals. Don't get me wrong. I like animals. But I felt like an alien in that Wild Life Safari Park, an alien who would shortly be discovered and meet his doom. It was the heat. It had to be the heat.

'Let's go somewhere cool to have our lunch,' I said. Mo was skipping along beside me and she stopped in mid-hop and peered at me. Then she gave the bag I was carrying to Jonathan.

'You have it,' she told him.

He started to say not likely, then changed his mind, I don't know why.

We began to climb out of the valley with its river, and away from the noise and up towards the hills. The bushes changed to trees and it grew cooler. I could breathe now.

'Not much further,' Mo called back. It seemed funny for her to be leading the way.

'Hurry up and stop soon,' Jill commanded, 'Or we'll be in Scotland at this rate.'

'Here. This is it,' called Mo.

Trees were all about us now, beeches and oaks, then fir trees. The ground was mossy, and last year's leaves still lay there. I dropped down and the ground was like velvet. No one said much as we opened our bags. I felt all right at last, except that I wanted to go to sleep.

'Wake me up when it's time to go. No, I don't want any food, you can have it. I only wanted a drink.'

That's when Mo said she didn't fancy sweets that looked like that.

'I thought we were having a game,' Jonathan said. 'I brought my ball with me.'

I wandered across the clearing to put down a couple of bags for goal posts, turning away from the others who were already kicking the ball around. Then, something pushed me, and I fell and hit my head on the root of a tree, hey presto, here we go, this is it, I thought, oh, no ...

Mo was bathing my head with orange juice and a paper towel when I struggled to sit up, which wasn't easy.

'Oh, you're all right,' said Jill, moving away to practise her football skills. Jonathan would have to look out or she'd be beating him.

'You'd best lie still,' Mo murmured. I agreed.

She went on bathing my head and I wasn't at all sure that it was doing any good but at least she cared which was more than the other two did, and then she wasn't bathing my head, and when I looked she was asleep.

I heard Jill shout, 'And I'm Witches United. What are you?' and I tried to pull myself up because for some reason I didn't like that at all, and I found I couldn't move, couldn't move an inch.

'Mo. Mo. Help me!' I screamed, not making a sound. And as my stomach quaked and trembled with terror I saw that Mo's eyes were open and that she was paralysed, too. I strained every muscle and there was nothing, nothing. But right in front of us stood a giant television set, that I somehow knew had been there all the time, framing trees that were in the wood and the screen too, and we were caught in those woods outside the screen, and as I watched, Jill and Jonathan left their game and walked through the trees and into the screen before us. And I screamed at them not to, but it was useless.

I think I saw the house before they did. I had known it across all those years at school, the gingerbread house covered with sweets of spun icing sugar in wonderful colours and stranger shapes, the sweets sent by my aunt Kate.

Then Jill and Jonathan saw the house and ran forward, breaking off pieces and pushing them into their mouths. After all that lunch, I thought angrily, they didn't have to start on the house. There's bound to be trouble. Soon there came a reedy whisper from inside,

'Who's that nibbling at my house?'

'Only the wind,' Jill replied, still chewing away like the starving.

She was always greedy, that girl. And a liar, as I've often pointed out, only nobody believes me.

And of course, the old witch came out of the house, just like I knew she would, and she was all you've ever wanted, green hooky nose, red shiny eyes, gruesome grey hair, a black hat and a tatty black cloak. Where had I seen her before? Oh, yes, of course, in the morning parcel from the Hartz Mountains where all the best witches live, and this looked like one of the Super Witch class, none of your getting-the-spells-mixed-up-wrong rubbish with this witch, anyone could see that. Pantomime land, fairy land here we come. I tried to laugh for after all it was a long, long time since we'd been in the Infants' listening to fairy tales. But I couldn't laugh, and anyway I could see Mo's face and she was scared silly.

'Come in, dearies,' the witch, kindly old dear herself, said to those two crazy idiots, my sister and my friend, and they looked at her as if she was nice, and went inside. How on earth could they, the stupid idiots? They'd still got use of their legs, hadn't they? Get out and run while you still can, I yelled at them, but I couldn't make a sound.

No, inside they went, smiling, and we followed them with our eyes, and we saw them eating up their supper of bread and honey and milk ... did that pair do nothing but eat? And then they went to their little white beds in their little rooms, blue for Jonathan, pink for Jill, stupid idiots.

As for Jonathan, what was he doing playing at being a German Hansel? He wasn't even the same colour, no type-casting there.

As in a play their night lasted for only a few of our minutes and then I saw Jill come down to breakfast. Not more food, surely? But for Jill the feasting was finished.

'Hansel, where are you?' she called and the witch came in and beat her with a stick, pointing at the broomstick and shouting until Jill got the message. Weeping, she began to clean the witch's house. The television camera panned over to where Jonathan was shut up in a cage, only a wooden one and I was sure he could have broken out of it if he'd known he was Jonathan, and the most powerful boy in the school; but at least he could still move fast, for the old woman started to poke at him with her stick through the bars of the cage and he scuttled to a corner to be out of the way. For the first time I realised how blind her red, piggy eyes were as she peered and squinted trying to see him and prod him. At last he seized something from the corner and held it out to her and she felt it with her claw-like hands, nodded to herself and went away. I knew what it was, of course; a bone.

'Jonathan,' I spoke, uselessly, and then I sent the strongest possible thought-wave over, but it couldn't have had much power for he stayed crouched in misery in the corner of the cage. So, 'Hansel,' I cried in my mind, very miserably, for if he thought he really was Hansel then we were all done for. But he didn't take any notice of that, either. 'Idiot. Goon. Nutter,' I next sent over angrily. How could anyone be so stupid?

The witch took to beating and pinching Jill again, and that and the tears sliding down Mo's face, which she couldn't wipe away, convinced me I had to do something. But what? And how? Beating Space Invaders had nothing on this crazy set-up.

Jill was crying and begging for food, which seemed a bit much to me till I remembered that we were in a time warp and they might have been the witch's captives for some days now. It's as bad as being a hostage, I thought wildly. The old woman cackled, a horrible, stagy kind of cackle that set your teeth on edge, and gave Jill an acorn. Jill started to scream and shout till the old woman hit her hard with the stick and she too, crawled to the corner and hid her face in her hands.

I had to break out of the paralysis that held me and shout to them that they could walk out of the television set at any time. Though surely, even if they thought they were Hansel and Gretel, not Jonathan and Jill, the story would end happily with the witch dead and the children finding the jewels ...

And it was then I began to feel horribly afraid because if they really thought they were Hansel and Gretel, then anything could happen. If they were still Jonathan and Jill they'd know the story ends happily because they're only in a play. But if the play was reality for them then they'd get nothing to remember because it was all happening for the first time and so the play could change to something different - to disaster. The witch might find out Jonathan was holding out a bone; Jill might not be strong enough to push her into the oven.

I tried to cry out, to warn them but no sound came. Frozen in a sleep-world dream-world I watched the witch bully Jill into cleaning the house, and when she discovered Jonathan in the cage her sobs were heart-rending. Tears were sliding down Mo's face and she couldn't wipe them away. We watched the grisly tale unfolding - Jill starved and beaten, sweeping, chopping wood, drawing water. The witch had obviously never heard of labour-saving devices.

Every day the old hag went to inspect Jonathan to see if he was fattening up yet, and he would hold out the bone for her and she would blink her red eyes and sigh, then grow irritable and poke at Jonathan with a stick, but he'd nip away so that she couldn't reach him. Then she would beat Jill and make her prepare food for Jonathan. Jill hardly tried to talk to him any more as she had at first, for all the Jill spirit was being knocked out of her as she turned into this Gretel creature.

I hoped the look of Jonathan would make her see that he wasn't a German Hansel and then she'd know and get out of this mad play. But no. And by now she seemed so tired I was scared the witch might prove too tough for her in the end.

Time went by and the end was coming.

One day the witch lost patience. She stormed into the kitchen and shrilled at Jill.

'Stoke up the fire. Heat up the grate. Fat or thin, I'll eat him today.'

And this was the moment. Could the weeping Gretel/Jill push her into the oven and make the big getaway? Of course she could. It was in the book, wasn't it? But she just looked pathetic standing there crying her eyes out.

'Jill, Jill. Push the old bag into the oven! Now!'

My mind rocked with the force I sent over. It must work, this time.

And the witch looked out of the telly straight at me and cackled gruesomely like a mad hyena hooked on laughing gas. My blood ran cold.

'Thank you! Thank you very, very much for warning me!'

She giggled loathesomely, her yellow teeth jutting out.

'It won't be me who'll bake in the oven, he, he, he!'

Panic struck. I'd made everything much, much worse. I tried to twist and turn out of the paralysis that held me. Somebody, somewhere, do something please. Jonathan, break out of that stupid cage. Wake up, Jill. Mo seemed to be praying. That's a good idea, I thought and came up with Please Saint Christopher, who looks after travellers, do something, anything about this awful school outing ... which wasn't what I meant to say at all.

But Mo moved. She crawled painfully to something that lay on the ground and flung it at the screen.

The world shimmered and shook like the hottest heat haze of all, then it rocked and turned making me feel very ill indeed. When it straightened once more, Jonathan stood over the football saying,

'You cheated. Not fair.'

There was no television set, no witch, only us and the trees all around us.

'I never cheat,' shouted Jill.

'I can move,' I cried out.

Jill didn't even bother to look round.

'Of course you can. Did y'think you were paralysed or something?' she shouted.

'You haven't changed.'

'Am I supposed to have done?'

'Don't you remember?'

'Remember what? Listen, if you can't talk sense, shut up. Come on, another go, Jonathan.'

'Mo. Mo. Surely you remember? The witch? The gingerbread house?'

She frowned a bit, which wasn't usual for Mo.

'There was something, but it slips away out of my mind when I try to grab hold of it.'

'They were in the witch's house and we were watching.'

'It's no good. I don't think you're very well, David. It's so hot. And I feel as if I've been crying, which is daft for I hardly every cry.'

'Gosh. It's almost two,' called out Jonathan. 'We'd better get a move on if we're gonna join the rest of the monkeys.'

I followed him, still in a daze.

'Don't hang about, Jill. What are you doing?'

'Looking for my witch. Mum said I'd lose it and I have.'

'It's over there. In bits,' I told her for I knew now what Mo had flung at the telly.

'Yes, here's a bit of the broomstick. Why, it's splintered. Jonathan, you big oaf, you must have trodden on it with your great feet.'

'Mo flung it at the other witch and saved you both, I said.

'Oh, no. He's off again. Absolutely bonkers. Pack it in, David.'

I didn't want to walk with them. I hung back and looked at the witchy fragments. And in the green grass glass sparkled. A broken bottle? The witch's jewels?

'I'm not bonkers,' I said to myself, knowing even then that I would be the only one to believe me, and set off after them.

Next day - I'd got German measles.

The Ceremony

by Martin Copus

There were four gangs at our school. Four real gangs, that is. Lots of the juniors made up pretend gangs and went round boasting about it, but we just ignored them. We seniors knew about gangs and that's why there were only four - one for each year of the seniors. Everyone wanted to be in their year gang - it was the best thing that could happen to you. Sometimes you'd laugh at them and say you didn't care. But that was just to make out you couldn't be bothered. All the time everyone was dying to be a gang member. I certainly was.

You could have as many as you liked in the gang but not just anyone could join. You had to be asked to join by a boy who was already a member. Of course, girls couldn't be members anyway, but they could join in with the gang outings if they weren't soppy. I had loads of friends in the gang. One of my best mates, Arthur, was Secretary to the gang, and that meant he counted who was at meetings and made sure things were done properly and that. Because of Arthur I knew a lot about the gang. I knew their secret meeting place, their secret sign. I even knew what they were going to do next. Arthur told me as we went home together after school each day. But that's all I knew. I didn't know what it was like to be in the gang, to be one of the chosen few. Mostly, though, I didn't know about the Ceremony. No matter how often I asked, Arthur would never say anything about that. And that's why I wasn't in the gang. I was frightened about the Ceremony.

We all knew that no-one could join the gang unless he passed an initiation rite. But all members were sworn to secrecy about it. All we knew was that everyone had to go through it and that it was horrible. So when I was asked to join I was dead scared. I pleaded with Arthur to tell me what I had to do. But he wouldn't say anything.

'Go on, Arthur. Please,' I said.

'No. I'm sworn to secrecy.'

'But you can tell me. I mean, I'll be a member soon.'

'That's right, and then you'll be sworn to secrecy.'

I was desperate. I had to know what the Ceremony was and Arthur was the only way I could find out.

'If you tell me ...' I went on.

'Yes?'

'I'll give you ... I'll give you my latest car!'

I'd always collected cars. But I was especially proud of my collection of matchbox toys. They were great. There was nobody in our street or school who could beat me. Everyone knew I had the best collection out. I'd just bought a new one from money I'd earned doing errands in the holidays. It had a new type of wheel which made it go faster. I was offering this to Arthur. I could see he wanted it, too.

He looked at me, and his eyes were all screwed up. I could see that I might get what I wanted. Then he said,

'Which new car?'

I explained. 'You've always wanted one of those, haven't you?'

'Yes,' he said.

'Well, you tell me about the Ceremony and you can have it.'

'No.'

'What?'

'No. I can't tell you. I'm sworn to secrecy.' And that was that.

All that evening I thought about the Ceremony. Arthur was one of my very best friends and I'd offered to give him my very best car. Yet he said he couldn't tell me. Now I knew the Ceremony must be really horrible. The gang must make a member swear to keep quiet on pain of something terrible. What could it be? I began to think of all the nasty things that the gang might do. I began to think I was already a member, but I had told another the secret of the Ceremony and the gang was after me. What would they do? Pull out my tongue? Stick pins under my nails? Ugh! I was really scared now. Tomorrow was the testing time. I'd have to go through the Ceremony then, after school. And, of course, no-one got a second chance.

My mum was ironing, so I asked her. I didn't ask her straight out. She'd only tell me I couldn't be a gang member, I knew that. I sort of mentioned belonging to things like the public library. I knew she wouldn't say anything about that, in fact, she said that it was a good idea to belong to the library. So far, so good. I started to fold up a few of the things she was ironing just to put her in a good mood, and asked a few general questions about this and that. Then I said,

'What sort of things do they do at ceremonies?'

'What ceremonies?'

'Well, any ceremonies.'

'Depends.'

'What does it depend on?'

'What sort of ceremony it is.'

'What d'you mean?'

'What do you mean, what do I mean?'

'Well, you know, what do they do at ceremonies?'

'Go and finish your tea.'

'I have finished.'

'Then watch the television.'

So I went and watched telly for a bit. But that didn't tell me anything about the Ceremony either. In the end, I had to go to bed to puzzle it out. When the light was out, I pulled the bedclothes over my head and imagined I was in a rabbit hole. Then I started to think about the Ceremony.

It couldn't be all that bad, I thought, because if it was really bad there wouldn't be any gang members. Now that was a cheering thought. No, it couldn't be so bad, because no-one would want to take it. Then I thought that it could be that bad because no-one ever knew that it was like until they took it and then it was too late to change their minds. In fact, the more I thought about it, wrapped in my woolly rabbit hole, the more I realised that it probably was absolutely, unspeakably horrible - and that was why no-one would speak about it.

I stuck my head out of the bedclothes and peered at my watch. The numbers and hands glowed in the dark. It said ten o'clock. School was at nine, I'd be woken up at seven. That left only nine hours for me to think about it. That wasn't very long, was it? Then I must have fallen asleep because it was morning. The day of the Ceremony had come.

The day of the Ceremony was just like any other day really. But all the time I felt as if something ought to happen. You know, something very unusual. At first I thought perhaps Miss Craddock, who took arithmetic, would be ill. But she wasn't. Then I wondered if someone would share their sandwiches with me. I had school dinners but sometimes people who had sandwiches would eat too many sweets and give their food away. But that didn't happen either. In fact, I soon knew that the day of the Ceremony was going to be just like any other day. And it was too, for everyone else.

Well, you know what I was thinking about all day. I tried to think about other things, but it was hopeless. So after dinner I just thought about nothing else. Then the bell went for the end of school. The moment I was dreading had arrived.

We all put our chairs up and went to the cloakroom. I was as quick as I could be. I felt cold all over. I went out to the playground. Arthur was waiting.

'Come on then,' and he grabbed me and pulled me out of the gate.

The gang was waiting round the corner. I knew only one or two. The others, about ten or so, were from different classes.

'This is him,' said Arthur, and they all looked at me as if I was the first person they'd ever seen. I smiled and tried to think up something funny to say. But they just walked round me and then, with me in the middle, the gang moved off down the road. Thanks to Arthur, I knew where we were going, but it was a strange going. Everybody was dead quiet, as if we were all going to a funeral. All I could hear was the screech of someone's shoes and the quiet tap of the gang's feet. It was eerie, and in a way that was worse than if they'd all been talking about me, because I was all by myself thinking about the Ceremony.

The secret meeting place was an old house on the edge of the railway. It was fenced off and there were big notices everywhere telling you to keep out. But the gang didn't keep out and nor did I. For the first time I squeezed under the wire too. I scratched the back of my leg and put my hand into a great load of stingers, but no-one said anything, so I didn't either, even though it hurt. I was secretly hoping the scratch would start pouring blood so they would all see how brave I was and let me off the Ceremony.

We went into the house by a broken window. Inside, it was dark and smelt like the hamster's cage at school. There were bits of newspaper all over the floor and bits of wallpaper were peeling off the walls. But the gang had put boxes and things in it to sit on. When we were all in they all sat down, but Arthur pushed me into the middle of the floor. Someone came up and tied a hanky over my eyes. I didn't like that at all.

'OK,' someone said, 'let it begin.'

I was grabbed and spun round and round. It was just like being in a game of blind man's bluff, except there were no giggling girls, and I felt wobbly with fear and spinning.

'He must answer the questions,' said the Voice. I recognised it was Georgie Dougan but it was all growly as if he was trying to be someone else. Then, one by one, they each asked me a question. They weren't hard questions, just things like what my name was and if I'd keep all the rules and die rather than give up the gang's secrets. I could answer them all, it was just that they shot them at me from different parts of the room until I wasn't sure if I'd answered the last question or the one before that. But at last it was over. They'd all asked a question.

'Enough,' said Georgie.

Well, I thought, that wasn't so bad. I wonder if I'm in, and I was starting to think that I'd done quite well, when Georgie said,

'Bring in the worms.'

Worms? Worms? What did they want worms for? Surely I'd passed the Ceremony? Why bring in worms?

It was Arthur who spoke next. And in a way it was because it was one of my best friends who said it that made it that bit worse.

'All you've got to do is eat these.'

My hands twitched and I was going to pull my blindfold off, but they were grabbed by hard fingers. I wriggled but couldn't do anything.

'Come on,' said Arthur. His voice was a bit quieter, more friendly and I knew he wanted me in.

I swallowed, but my throat was dry and it hurt. Something cold and slimy touched my lips. Ugh! My insides rolled over and my mouth filled with bitter tasting water. I opened my mouth and fingers pushed in a worm. I felt its cold body slide down my throat. Now I felt I really would be sick. I couldn't swallow, but fingers were already pushing in another. Together they went down. All I could taste were the dirty fingers that tasted of bike oil. It was horrible but at least it stopped me thinking of the worms. I coughed and spat out the taste.

'That's it then,' said Georgie.

'Well done,' said Arthur, 'you're one of us now.'

A few others said, 'Well done', too. My hands were let go and I took off the blindfold. Everyone was grinning and I felt a lovely warm glow come over me. For the first time I realised just how scared I'd been. They all started to chat at once and I was one of the gang.

A fat boy came up to me. He held a dirty old spaghetti tin in his hand and I saw that his fingers were all oily.

'You were very brave,' he said and I laughed with happiness.

I was really glad to see what I'd been eating. It was a good trick though. You try it for yourself - cold spaghetti feels just like worms when you put it in your mouth. I was blindfolded and dizzy too.

On the way home I was still excited. I couldn't believe that I'd really done it. All that worrying and being really scared and at last I'd passed the Ceremony. I was in.

Arthur was chatting to me friendlier than ever. I felt I had to tell him what I'd really felt like.

'You know,' I said, and I tried to sound as if I was dead calm, 'for a bit I thought they were real.'

'What?'

'The spaghetti from the tin. I thought they were real worms.'

'You're soft.'

'Yeah, but I soon realised and when I saw the tin, well, then I knew.'

'No, you great fool. You're soft if you think it was spaghetti. That was just the tin we collect the worms in.'

A Mother in Mannville

by Marjorie Kinnan Rawlings

The orphanage is high in the Carolina mountains. Sometimes in winter the snowdrifts are so deep that the institution is cut off from the village below, from all the world. Fog hides the mountain peaks, the snow swirls down the valleys, and a wind blows so bitterly that the orphanage boys who take the milk twice daily to the baby cottage reach the door with fingers stiff in an agony of numbness.

'Or when we carry trays from the cookhouse for the ones that are sick,' Jerry said, 'we get our faces frostbit, because we can't put our hands over them. I have gloves,' he added. 'Some of the boys don't have any.'

He liked the late spring, he said. The rhododendron was in bloom, a carpet of colour, across the mountainsides, soft as the May winds that stirred the hemlocks. He called it laurel.

'It's pretty when the laurel blooms,' he said. 'Some of it's pink and some of it's white.'

I was there in autumn. I wanted quiet, isolation, to do some troublesome writing. I wanted mountain air to blow out the malaria from too long a time in the subtropics. I was homesick, too, for the flaming of maples in October, and for corn shocks and pumpkins and black-walnut trees and the lift of hills. I found them all, living in a cabin that belonged to the orphanage, half a mile beyond the orphanage farm. When I took the cabin, I asked for a boy or man to come and chop wood for the fireplace. The first few days were warm, I found what wood I needed about the cabin, no one came, and I forgot the order.

I looked up from my typewriter one late afternoon, a little startled. A boy stood at the door, and my pointer dog, my companion, was at his side and had not barked to warn me. The boy was probably twelve years old, but undersized. He wore overalls and a torn shirt, and was barefooted.

He said, 'I can chop some wood today.'

I said, 'But I have a boy coming from the orphanage.'

'I'm the boy.'

'You? But you're small.'

'Size don't matter, chopping wood,' he said. 'Some of the big boys don't chop good. I've been chopping wood at the orphanage a long time.'

I visualized mangled and inadequate branches for my fire. I was well into my work and not inclined to conversation. I was a little blunt.

'Very well. There's the axe. Go ahead and see what you can do.'

I went back to work, closing the door. At first the sound of the boy dragging brush annoyed me. Then he began to chop. The blows were rhythmic and steady, and shortly I had forgotten him, the sound no more of an interruption than a consistent rain. I suppose an hour and a half passed, for when I stopped and stretched, and heard the boy's steps on the cabin stoop, the sun was dropping behind the farthest mountain, and the valleys were purple with something deeper than the asters.

The boy said, 'I have to go to supper now. I can come again tomorrow evening.'

I said, 'I'll pay you now for what you've done,' thinking I should probably have to insist on an older boy. 'Ten cents an hour?'

'Anything is all right.'

We went together back of the cabin. An astonishing amount of solid wood had been cut. There were cherry logs and heavy roots of rhododendron, and blocks from the waste pine and oak left from the building of the cabin.

'But you've done as much as a man,' I said. 'This is a splendid pile.'

I looked at him, actually, for the first time. His hair was the colour of the corn shocks, and his eyes, very direct, were like the mountain sky when rain is pending - grey, with a showing of that miraculous blue. As I spoke a light came over him, as though the setting sun had touched him with the same suffused glory with which it touched the mountains. I gave him a quarter.

'You may come tomorrow,' I said, 'and thank you very

much.'

He looked at me, and at the coin, and seemed to want to speak, but could not, and turned away.

'I'll split the kindling tomorrow,' he said over his thin ragged shoulder. 'You'll need kindling and medium wood and logs and backlogs.'

At daylight I was half awakened by the sound of chopping. Again it was so even in texture that I went back to sleep. When I left my bed in the cool morning, the boy had come and gone, and a stack of kindling was neat against the cabin wall. He came again after school in the afternoon and worked until time to return to the orphanage. His name was Jerry; he was twelve years old, and he had been at the orphanage since he was four. I could picture him at four, with the same grave grey-blue eyes and the same - independence? No, the word that comes to me is integrity.

The word means something very special to me, and the quality for which I use it is a rare one. My father had it - there is another of whom I am almost sure - but almost no man of my acquaintance possesses it with the clarity, the purity, the simplicity of a mountain stream. But the boy Jerry had it. It is bedded on courage, but it is more than brave. It is honest, but it is more than honesty. The axe handle broke one day. Jerry said the woodshop at the orphanage would repair it. I brought money to pay for the job and he refused it.

'I'll pay for it,' he said. 'I broke it. I brought the axe down careless.'

'But no-one hits accurately every time,' I told him. 'The fault was in the wood of the handle. I'll see the man from whom I bought it.'

It was only then that he would take the money. He was standing back of his own carelessness. He was a free-will agent and he chose to do careful work, and if he failed, he took the responsibility without subterfuge.

And he did for me the unnecessary thing, the gracious

thing, that we find done only by the great of heart. Things no training can teach, for they are done on the instant, with no predicated experience. He found a cubbyhole beside the fireplace that I had not noticed. There, of his own accord, he put kindling and medium wood, so that I might always have dry fire material ready in case of sudden wet weather. A stone was loose in the rough walk to the cabin. He dug a deeper hole and steadied it, although he came, himself, by a short cut over the bank. I found that when I tried to return his thoughtfulness with such things as candy and apples, he was wordless. 'Thank you' was, perhaps, an expression for which he had had no use, for his courtesy was instinctive. He only looked at the gift and at me, and a curtain lifted, so that I saw deep into the clear well of his eyes, and gratitude was there, and affection, soft over the firm granite of his character.

He made simple excuses to come and sit with me. I could no more have turned him away than if he had been physically hungry. I suggested once that the best time for us to visit was just before supper, when I left off my writing. After that, he waited always until my typewriter had been some time quiet. One day I worked until nearly dark. I went outside the cabin, having forgotten him. I saw him going up over the hill in the twilight toward the orphanage. When I sat down on my stoop, a place was warm from his body where he had been sitting.

He became intimate, of course, with my pointer, Pat. There is a strange communion between a boy and a dog. Perhaps they possess the same singleness of spirit, the same kind of wisdom. It is difficult to explain, but it exists. When I went across the state for a weekend I left the dog in Jerry's charge. I gave him the dog whistle and the key to the cabin, and left sufficient food. He was to come two or three times a day and let out the dog, and feed and exercise him. I should return Sunday night, and Jerry would take out the dog for the last time Sunday afternoon and then leave the key under an agreed hiding place.

My return was belated and fog filled the mountain passes so treacherously that I dared not drive at night. The fog held the next morning, and it was Monday noon before I reached the cabin. The dog had been fed and cared for that morning. Jerry came early in the afternoon, anxious.

'The superintendent said nobody would drive in the fog,' he said. 'I came just before bedtime last night and you hadn't come. So I brought Pat some of my breakfast this morning. I wouldn't have let anything happen to him.'

'I was sure of that. I didn't worry.'

'When I heard about the fog, I thought you'd know.'

He was needed for work at the orphanage and he had to return at once. I gave him a dollar in payment, and he looked at it and went away. But that night he came in the darkness and knocked at the door.

'Come in, Jerry,' I said, 'if you're allowed to be away this late.'

'I told maybe a story,' he said. 'I told them I thought you would want to see me.'

'That's true,' I assured him, and I saw his relief. 'I want to hear about how you managed with the dog.'

He sat by the fire with me, with no other light, and told me of their two days together. The dog lay close to him, and found a comfort there that I did not have for him. And it seemed to me that being with my dog, and caring for him, had brought the boy and me, too, together, so that he felt that he belonged to me as well as to the animal.

'He stayed right with me,' he told me, 'except when he ran in the laurel. He likes the laurel. I took him up over the hill and we both ran fast. There was a place where the grass was high and I lay down in it and hid. I could hear Pat hunting for me. He found my trail and he barked. When he found me, he acted crazy, and he ran around and around me, in circles.'

We watched the flames.

'That's an apple log,' he said. 'It burns the prettiest of any wood.'

We were very close.

He was suddenly impelled to speak of things he had not spoken of before, nor had I cared to ask him.

'You look a little bit like my mother,' he said. 'Especially in the dark, by the fire.'

'But you were only four, Jerry, when you came here. You have remembered how she looked, all these years?'

'My mother lives in Mannville,' he said.

For a moment, finding that he had a mother shocked me as greatly as anything in my life has ever done, and I did not know why it disturbed me. Then I understood my distress. I was filled with a passionate resentment that any woman should go away and leave her son. A fresh anger added itself. A son like this one ... The orphanage was a wholesome place, the executives were kind, good people, the food was more than adequate, the boys were healthy, a ragged shirt was no hardship, nor the doing of clean labour. Granted, perhaps, that the boy felt no lack, what about the mother? At four he would have looked the same as now. Nothing, I thought, nothing in life could change those eyes. His quality must be apparent to an idiot, a fool. I burned with questions I could not ask. In any, I was afraid, there would be pain.

'Have you seen her, Jerry - lately?'

'I see her every summer. She sends for me.'

I wanted to cry out. 'Why are you not with her? How can she let you go away again?'

He said, 'She comes up here from Mannville whenever she can. She doesn't have a job now.'

His face shone in the firelight.

'She wanted to give me a puppy, but they can't let any one boy keep a puppy. You remember the suit I had on last Sunday?' He was plainly proud. 'She sent me that for Christmas. The Christmas before that' - he drew a long breath, savouring the memory - 'she sent me a pair of skates.'

'Roller skates?'

My mind was busy, making pictures of her, trying to understand her. She had not, then, entirely deserted or forgotten him. But why, then - I thought, 'But I must not condemn her without knowing.'

'Roller skates. I let the other boys use them. They're always borrowing them. But they're careful of them.'

What circumstances other than poverty ...

'I'm going to take the dollar you gave me for taking care of Pat,' he said, 'and buy her a pair of gloves.'

I could only say, 'That will be nice. Do you know her size?'

'I think it's eight and a half,' he said.

He looked at my hands.

'Do you wear eight and a half?' he asked.

'No. I wear a smaller size, a six.'

'Oh! Then I guess her hands are bigger than yours.'

I hated her. Poverty or no, there was other food than bread, and the soul could starve as quickly as the body. He was taking his dollar to buy gloves for her big stupid hands, and she lived away from him, in Mannville, and contented herself with sending him skates.

'She likes white gloves,' he said. 'Do you think I can get them for a dollar?'

'I think so,' I said.

I decided that I should not leave the mountains without seeing her and knowing for myself why she had done this thing.

The human mind scatters its interests as though made of thistledown, and every wind stirs and moves it. I finished my work. It did not please me, and I gave my thoughts to another field. I should need some Mexican material.

I made arrangements to close my Florida place. Mexico immediately, and doing the writing there, if conditions were favourable. Then, Alaska with my brother. After that, heaven knew what or where.

I did not take time to go to Mannville to see Jerry's mother, nor even to talk with the orphanage officials about her. I was a trifle abstracted about the boy, because of my work and plans. And after my first fury at her - we did not speak of her again - his having a mother, any sort at all, not far away, in Mannville, relieved me of the ache I had had about him. He did not question the anomalous relation. He was not lonely. It was none of my concern.

He came every day and cut my wood and did small helpful favours and stayed to talk. The days had become cold, and often I let him come inside the cabin. He would lie on the floor in front of the fire, with one arm across the pointer, and they would both doze and wait quietly for me. Other days they ran with a common ecstasy through the laurel, and since the asters were now gone, he brought me back vermilion maple leaves, and chestnut boughs dripping with imperial yellow. I was ready to go.

I said to him, 'You have been my good friend, Jerry. I shall often think of you and miss you. Pat will miss you too. I am leaving tomorrow.'

He did not answer. When he went away, I remember that a new moon hung over the mountains, and I watched him go in silence up the hill. I expected him the next day, but he did not come. The details of packing my personal belongings, loading my car, arranging the bed over the seat, where the dog would ride, occupied me until late in the day. I closed the cabin and started the car, noticing that the sun was in the west and I should do well to be out of the mountains by nightfall. I stopped by the orphanage and left the cabin key and money for my light bill with Miss Clark.

'And will you call Jerry for me to say goodbye to him?'

'I don't know where he is,' she said. 'I'm afraid he's not well. He didn't eat his dinner this noon. One of the boys saw him going over the hill into the laurel. He was supposed to fire the boiler this afternoon. It's not like him; he's unusually reliable.'

I was almost relieved, for I knew I should never see him again, and it would be easier not to say goodbye to him.

I said, 'I wanted to talk with you about his mother - why

he's here - but I'm in more of a hurry than I expected to be. It's out of the question for me to see her now. But here's some money I'd like to leave with you to buy things for him at Christmas and on his birthday. It will be better than for me to try to send him things. I could so easily duplicate - skates, for instance.'

She blinked her honest spinster's eyes.

'There's not much use for skates here,' she said.

Her stupidity annoyed me.

'What I mean,' I said, 'is that I don't want to duplicate things his mother sends him. I might have chosen skates if I didn't know she had already given them to him.'

'I don't understand,' she said. 'He has no mother. He has no skates.'

Yellow Bird

by John Latham

I was nine. Mrs Mallion was visiting her sister, in Bootle, for a few days - the first time she'd slept away from Kingsley in her life. Mr Mallion had died a few months before. 'Now Bill's pushin' up th'daisies I may as well see summat o'the rest o'the world', she said. 'Gi'us a bit to chew on when I join him. Long time down theer. We'll need plenty to yossack about!'

My mother had helped her pack, made her sandwiches for the complicated bus journey, persuaded her she needn't take her curling tongs, promised to look after her house. We walked with her along the road, staggering under the weight of three gigantic fruit cakes and a couple of chickens she'd killed and roasted the night before. 'There'll be somebody at t'other end to help me lommer it', she said. There always was. When my mother and I got home from the bus stop we found a fruit cake and a chicken in the porch.

One of the jobs was to feed Joey, Mrs Mallion's old canary. Each day she was away, I went with my mother to help. The bird would sit for hours on Mrs Mallion's shoulder, while the old lady was knitting, but my mother thought we'd better not let it out. I tried hard, but couldn't persuade her to.

On the fifth day, my mother was rather harrassed because Auntie Jill and her cousin Elsie - the only person I knew who drank tea with lemon in - had come round unexpectedly. 'Do you think you could feed Joey before you go to play?', she asked. I jumped at the chance. Mrs Mallion's door was never locked. 'If some poor beggar wants anythin' I've got, thers welcome!'. Joey seemed pleased to see me, and trilled while I changed the water, added seed.

I had to do it. I opened the door of the cage and inserted my hand, index finger crooked, like the picture of St Francis in my Bible-study book. To my surprise Joey backed away, but as I advanced further he dived out with a whirr of wings, his feathers flicking my face. When I turned round, he was sitting on the curtain rail.

I wanted Joey on my shoulder. I couldn't reach him from the chair, so I climbed onto the windowsill, stood on tiptoe. I was still a few inches too low. I leapt and the bird hopped sideways out of reach. I tried several times, with no success. Then I saw my mother rushing down the road, probably off to buy a lemon from Alick's. I yanked the curtain round me, but she didn't look up. Even so, I daren't climb on the windowsill again. I'd have to find some new strategy. I was growing rather cross with Joey.

Mrs Mallion had laid the fire for her return. Screws of newspaper protruded from the bars. I tried to read the words on them. '... ales in dang ...', one crumpled message said.

I was proud of my reading. Only Marlene in our class was better. What did it mean? Ales, I knew, were bitter drinks that came in brown bottles. My father kept some by the piano, and once in a while, if I came down early, an empty one would be standing on top. I'd tilt it back, catch a drop or two. I always hated it.

Dang I wasn't sure about. It sounded like a clock, or more probably a bell. A bell full of ale. Perhaps the church in a brewery had been flooded. It wouldn't ring properly. If there was any noise at all, it would just be a sad, drowned clack. But there probably wouldn't be any, like when I tried to blow my whistle in the bath. No sound at all, but some lovely patterns in the bubbles. What a silly story to put in the newspaper!

I had to crane my neck to read '... feat of Hitler ...' I tried to imagine them. Mr Aston, at Sunday school, had described the devil. Mrs Capper said that Hitler was the very devil. The biggest devil, I supposed that meant. A cloven foot like beasts, Mr Aston said. 'Craven A' my father smoked, in a packet the colour of blood. Raven tearing sheep, goose-stepping in his cloven feet. Why didn't they fly away? Heels clacking. Hens. Ducks. His funny moustache, singed in Hell. A puzzling story.

A box of matches was lying on the range. I opened it.

Pink heads to the north, black ones to the south, no arms at all, like the boys and girls in hospital when we had our tonsils out, and we slept four to a bed because of all the men brought in, burned when the gasometer was bombed. That devil, Hitler!

I'd never struck a match. I took one out, ran it along the sandpaper. The sound made my teeth grate. There was a flurry of sparks, but it didn't light. I tried again. It broke in half as it flared, then fell onto my foot. I stamped it out. Finally I succeeded, and applied it to one of the screws of paper, in the way I'd seen my mother do.

A lick of flame ran between the bars, cast a yellow shadow on the kindling. Soon the fire was roaring. It was perfectly safe. If I didn't put coal on it would go out soon, and later, when it was cold, I'd build it up again. No one would ever know.

I sat in the rocking chair and watched it. I loved the way the paper burned. First a tinge of brown, the words dark and solemn, then a deeper patch spreading steadily across, a burst of flame - then a shimmering residue, frail and thin, the letters a dull silver, like angels or ancient bones. There were some logs stacked by the coal scuttle. I threw one on. It wouldn't take long to burn.

I remembered Joey. He was still perched on the curtain rail, not singing. He didn't look grateful at all. Now I had to catch him, put him back. In the kitchen I found a feather duster on a long cane handle. The duster was no use, but the cane would be, if I could find a net or bag to fasten to the other end. I came across a hairnet in the sideboard drawer. Ideal! I fastened it to the cane with garden twine, crept up to the curtains and swung it. Joey hopped to the side, just before the hairnet hit the rail. I tried again. Joey hopped back to his original position. He looked contemptuously at the ceiling.

I lost my temper, swung the cane swiftly along the rail. Joey hopped over it and settled again. I swished it furiously back. The net grazed Joey, who flew across the room, seemed to hit the wall, but clung onto the picture rail, just as inaccessible as before. I sneaked across the carpet, swung again, and perhaps because he was dazed or too confident, I caught him. He fluttered wildly in the net, but he was trapped.

I lowered the cane, inch by inch, until the net was in front of me. Joey was motionless. Perhaps he was reconciled. I slid my hand inside the net. He dug his beak into my upturned wrist. It was hurting but I grabbed him and pulled him out. His chest was fibrillating wildly, but his wings were still. I placed him on my shoulder, still holding him. He didn't struggle. I let go, and he shot across the room again, collided with the curtain, clung on to it.

'Cheat!', I yelled. I was furious. I grabbed the cane and swung it. It hit the curtain just below him. He zoomed off, hit the mirror, ricocheted, and while I was whirling he screeched past me, wing brushing my hair, and flew straight into the fire.

There was a dreadful dry crackling sound, a puff of yellow flame, the frantic flutter of shrivelling wings, a faint whiff of roasting - and then all I could see was a claw curling, turning orange, slipping down underneath a log. I was violently sick, all over Mrs Mallion's best carpet.

The next few hours were terrible. I cleaned up the mess and pleaded with God to bring Joey back. Each time I saw his cage I was convulsed with sobbing. I burned my wrist badly, raking out the fire before it was properly cool. It took all my courage, but I found no sign of Joey except the brass ring Mr Mallion had fastened round his leg.

I couldn't confess to her, she was so fond of the bird. But she was short-sighted, and if I could replace him, perhaps she wouldn't notice. I sneaked home, rifled my moneybox, and Geoff's. Twenty-one pence, altogether. I crept down again, but my mother had heard me. 'Did you feed Joey?' 'Yes!', I yelled. 'Thanks, love'.

I raced down the street to Mr Simpson's. He was just about to shut up shop. 'Please', I gasped. 'I need a yellow bird. 'I've got twenty-one p.' 'Why don't you come back tomorrow, son? You'll have more time to look around'. 'It's got to be today!', I exclaimed. He could tell I was on the verge of tears. 'Right!', he said. 'Come and see'.

I'd loved his aviary when I'd been before, but now I didn't notice it. All I wanted was a yellow bird. Already, I couldn't remember exactly what Joey had looked like, but none of the birds were right. One, however, seemed closer than the rest. Smaller, perhaps, with a stripe of blue, but maybe Mrs Mallion wouldn't notice. 'Can I have that one, please? How much is it?' 'Twenty-one pence', Mr Simpson said. That was lucky! He lent me a small cage to carry it away in.

I didn't want anyone to see me, especially not with the bird, so I stuffed the cage up my shirt and walked back up the hill by the quietest route, on the gravestone side of Church Entry. I was lucky and met no-one. I was dreadfully relieved to sneak into her house, particularly since the bird kept pecking my stomach. I put the cages together, slid the door of the small one with infinite care. The bird hopped onto Joey's perch. I closed the door. Then I closed my eyes. 'Thank you, God', I said.

The carpet was clean. The fire looked just as it had before I lit it. I put the duster and the hairnet away. Apart from the canaries, nothing had changed. Perhaps it would work out all right. I looked again at the bird. The blue stripe winked at me. She was bound to notice. My paints! Once more I sneaked into my house. I found my paint-box, stole out again.

The yellow was a little too light, so I added orange. Perfect! I spread it thickly on my brush, slid it through the bars of the cage. I'd almost touched the stripe when the bird took the brush in its beak and wrenched it. It daubed the perch with yellow as it fell to the floor of the cage. I cursed, retrieved it, went to the sink and washed the seeds away. The second time the canary jumped just as I reached it, and the brush moved smoothly along the length of its leg, coating it beautifully. Diddle diddle dumpling.

I gave up. Mrs Mallion probably wouldn't notice, and my burned wrist was hurting badly. I packed up my paints and went home. I told my mother I'd scraped my wrist on a rock. She looked uncertain, but put cream and a bandage on. It felt better. I told her I felt ill and couldn't eat. I just wanted to go to bed. After some argument she let me. I fell asleep straight away.

It was dark when I awoke, screaming. In the dream Hitler was frying Mr Mallion in a pan. Mr Mallion wouldn't stop laughing. His wings kept curling up into a scroll, then opening suddenly again. Hitler was shouting, spewing yellow saliva. When it landed in the pan it crackled, and Mr Mallion laughed louder. It was the crackling that made me scream.

Geoff, beside me, woke up, terrified, then shouted 'Mum. Jimmy's wet the bed!' I had. The sheet was still steaming. I was shivering uncontrollably. She raced upstairs, put her arms around me, rocked me until I was calm. Then very efficiently she changed the sheet and my pyjamas, tucked us in again. 'Baby!', whispered Geoff, and fell asleep again. She stayed with me, holding my hand.

In the nightmare that came later, I was in a paper bag and a giant was trying to stamp on me. I rolled this way and that, twisting, wriggling violently, but my feet were tied, and the only warning I had each time was the shadow as the foot stamped down. When it hit the paper bag, it crackled.

This time my screaming and the bed-wetting didn't wake my brother. My father came upstairs, as well. While my mother held me, and Geoff sucked his thumb, he put a towel underneath the wet part of the sheet - we hadn't another one - and folded it back. He said nothing while my mother rocked me.

When the hysteria had gone and I was sobbing quietly, he lifted me from her, sat on the bed and put me on his knee, facing him. This was strange. We'd seemed hardly to have touched each other for a long time, except for a clumsy ruffling of my hair - or my hand in his, at the end of a long walk, if Geoff was holding my mother's. 'Tell me what's the matter', he said, quite sternly. This was a shock after my mother's gentleness. 'Nothing', I sobbed. 'Just a terrible dream'. 'Don't lie!', he commanded. He was almost shouting, his grip on my arms was fierce. 'Tell me what happened! Now!'

I fell apart. I flung myself round his neck and poured it out, incoherently, with pauses filled with great convulsions. Now, he was wonderfully gentle, while at the same time his strength was protecting me. He held his face to mine. I felt the rough warmth of the whiskers I thought I'd grown too old for.

His anger had opened the floodgates. His love held them open while all the agony was emptying away. Peace crept over me. As I fell asleep, he kissed me on the forehead, lifted me. 'He can sleep in our bed', he said. 'Yes', replied my mother. 'I was thinking of having an early night'.

My only dread now was meeting Mrs Mallion. My father said I had to go. She'd been home for a few hours when I went round. My mother had met her off the bus, so I knew she would have told her.

'Come in, lad!', she said. 'Sit down'. She brought me a glass of her home-made ginger beer, and a slice of walnut cake. 'I hear you've bought me a present'. I tried to speak, but I burst into tears. She knelt down in front of me, drew me into her enormous bosom. It was warm and safe, and smelled of hens. When I subsided she clambered to her feet, puffing hard.

'That's enough o' t' watterworks', she said. 'Y'won't like yer cake if it's soggy! Now listen! I were fond o' Joey.' Tears started to prick again. 'And I hadn't heart to put him down. But he was sick, y'know. Tuberculosis. An' you put him out of his pain. And as for this one.' She indicated the new bird. 'He's a prize-winner! One yeller leg and one brown. I've got him entered for the Kingsley show!'

The Firework Display

by George Layton

Norbert was hanging from this branch, swinging his legs about, and trying to break it off. If the Park Ranger had come by and seen him, we'd all have been in trouble. Barry got hold of him round the ankles.

'Norbert, I'll do you if you don't come down.'

Norbert pulled his legs free, and moved along the branch towards the trunk. Barry chased after him and tried to pull him down again, but Norbert had managed to hoist himself up on to his tummy and was kicking Barry away.

'Gerroff!'

Barry punched him on the back of his leg.

'Well, get down then, or you'll get us all into trouble. Park Rangers said we could only take dead stuff.'

We were collecting for Bonfire Night. We were going to have the biggest bonfire in the district. It was already about twelve feet high, and it was only Saturday, so there were still two days to go. Three if you counted Monday itself.

We'd built the fire in Belgrave Street where the Council were knocking all the houses down. There was tons of waste ground, so there was no danger, and we'd found two old sofas and three armchairs to throw on the fire.

Norbert dropped from the branch and landed in some dog dirt. Barry and me laughed because he got it on his hands. I told him it served him right for trying to break the branch.

'You're stupid, Norbert. You know the Park Ranger said we could only take the dead branches.'

Norbert was wiping his hands on the grass.

'I thought it was dead.'

I threw a stick at him.

'How could it be dead if it's still growing? You're crackers you are, Norbert.'

The stick caught him on his shoulder. It was only a twig.

'Don't you throw lumps of wood at me! How would you like it if I threw lumps of wood at you?'

'Don't be so soft, Norbert, it was only a twig.'

Norbert picked up a big piece of wood, and chucked it at

me. Luckily it missed by miles.

'You're mad, Norbert. You want to be put away. You're a blooming maniac.'

'You started it. You shouldn't have chucked that stick at me.'

He went back to wiping his hands on the grass.

'Was it heckers like a stick. It was a little twig, and it's no good wiping your hands on the grass, you'll never get rid of that pong.'

Suddenly, Norbert ran at me, waving his hands towards my face. I got away as fast as I could but he kept following.

'If you touch me with those smelly hands ... I'm warning you, Norbert!'

I picked up a brick, and threatened him with it.

'I'm telling you, Norbert ...'

Just then I heard a voice from behind me.

'Hey!'

It was the Park Ranger.

'You lads, stop acting the goat. You!'

He meant me.

'What do you think you're doing with that?'

'Nowt ...'

I dropped the brick on the ground.

'... Just playing.'

'That's how accidents are caused. Now come on, lads, you've got your bonfire wood. On your way now.'

I gave Norbert another look, just to let him know that I'd meant it. He sniffed his hands.

'They don't smell, anyway.'

Barry and me got hold of the bottom branches and started dragging the pile, and Barry told Norbert to follow on behind.

'Norbert, you pick up anything that falls off, and chuck it back on. Come on, Tony and Trevor'll be wondering where we are.'

Trevor Hutchinson and Tony were back at Belgrave Street

guarding the fire. You had to do that to stop other lads from nicking all the wood you'd collected, or from setting fire to it. Not that it mattered, because if they did we'd just nick somebody else's.

Mind you, I wouldn't have been bothered if our fire had gone up in smoke, because it didn't look like my mum was going to let me go on Monday anyway. And even if she did, she certainly wouldn't let me have my own fireworks. I'd been on at her all morning about it while she'd been ironing.

'But why, Mum? All the other lads at school are having their own fireworks, all of 'em. Why can't I?'

Why was my mum so difficult? Why did she have to be so old-fashioned?

'Go on, Mum ...'

She just carried on with her ironing.

'It washes well this shirt.'

It was that navy blue one my Auntie Doreen had given me for my birthday.

'I'd like to get you another one. I must ask your Auntie Doreen where she bought it.'

'Why can't I have my own fireworks, Mum? Why?'

She just wouldn't listen.

'I'm old enough aren't I?'

'Will you remind me there's a button missing off this shirt?'

'Aren't I?'

'I don't know what you do with the buttons off your shirts. You must eat them.'

She was driving me mad.

'Mum, are you going to let me have my own fireworks this year or not?'

She slammed the iron down.

'Oh, stop mithering will you? You're driving me mad.'

'Well are you or aren't you?'

She put the shirt on a pile, and pulled a sheet out of the washing basket.

'No! You'll come with me and your Auntie Doreen to the firework display at the Children's Hospital like you do every year, and if you don't stop mithering you won't even be doing that. Now give me a hand with this.'

She game me one end of the sheet and we shook it.

'It's not fair. Tony's having his own fireworks this year, and he's three weeks younger than me, and Trevor Hutchinson's mum and dad have got him a £5 box.'

We folded the sheet twice to make it easier to iron.

'Then they've got more money than sense, that's all I can say.'

'I'll pay you back out of my spending money, honest.'

My mum gave me one of her looks.

'Oh yes? Like you did with your bike? One week you kept that up. I'm still waiting for the rest.'

That wasn't fair, it was ages ago.

'That's not fair, that was ages ago.'

I'd promised my mum that if she bought me a new bike, a drop handle-bar, I'd pay her some back every week out of my spending money. But she didn't give me enough. How could I pay her back?

'You don't give me enough spending money. I don't have enough to pay you back.'

'Why don't you save some? You don't have to spend it all do you?'

Bloomin' hummer! What's the point of calling it spending money, if you don't spend it?

'Mum, it's called spending money, isn't it? That means it's for spending. If it was meant for saving, people would call it saving money. You're only trying to get out of it.'

I was fed up. My mum was only trying to get out of getting me fireworks. She came over.

'Don't you be so cheeky, young man. Who do you think you're talking to?'

I thought for a minute she was going to clout me one.

'Well, even if I had some money saved, you wouldn't let me buy fireworks, would you?'

She didn't say anything.

'Well would you ... Eh?'

She told me not to say 'Eh' because it's rude. I don't think it's rude. It's just a word.

'Well, would you, Mum? If I had my own money, I bet you wouldn't let me buy fireworks with it.'

'Stop going on about it, for goodness' sake. You're not having any fireworks and that's final.'

It blooming well wasn't final. I wanted my own fireworks this year and that was final. Blimey, kids much younger than me have their own fireworks. Why shouldn't I?

'Apart from being a waste of money, they're dangerous.'

Dangerous. Honest, she's so old-fashioned, my mum.

'Mum, there are instructions on every firework. As long as you light the blue touch paper and retire, they're not dangerous.'

She started going on about how many people were taken to hospital every Bonfire Night, and how many children were injured, and how many limbs were lost, and if all fireworks were under supervised care like they are at the Children's Hospital, then there'd be far less accidents. She went on and on. I'd heard it all before.

'But I'll be careful, Mum, I promise. Please let me have my own fireworks.'

That's when she clouted me.

'Are you going deaf or summat?'

'What?'

It was Norbert shouting from behind.

'Y' what, Norbert?'

He picked up a branch that had fallen off, and threw it back on the pile.

'I've asked you twice. How many fireworks have you got? I've got over two pounds' worth, so far.'

Trust Norbert to start on about fireworks again. He knew I hadn't got any, because we'd talked about it the day before. Barry didn't help either.

'I've got about two pounds' worth an' all, and my dad says he might get me some more.'

It wasn't fair. I bet if I had a dad, I'd have plenty of fireworks. It wasn't fair.

'My mum hasn't got mine yet.'

Norbert snorted. He's always doing that.

'Huh, I bet she won't get you none either. She didn't last year. She wouldn't even let you come.'

'That was last year, wasn't it? She's getting me some this year.'

If only she was.

'Well, she'd better be quick, they're selling out. They've hardly got any left at Robinson's.'

Robinson's is the toy shop we all go to. Paul Robinson used to be in our class, but about two years back he was badly injured by a car. He doesn't go to our school any more. We see him sometimes in the holidays, but he doesn't seem to remember us.

'All right, all right, don't panic, she's getting them this morning, isn't she? She ordered them ages ago.'

I don't think Norbert believed me.

'Oh ... How many is she getting you?'

He isn't half a pest, Norbert. He goes on and on.

'I don't know. I'll see when I get home at dinner time.'

When we got back to Belgrave Street, Tony was throwing stones up in the air, seeing how high he could get them, and Trevor was riding round on my bike. There were stones and bits of glass all over the place.

'Hey, Trevor, gerroff! You'll puncture it.'

I took my bike off him, and leaned it against a rusty oil drum. Tony started to load the wood on to the fire.

'You've been ages. What took you so long? It's nearly dinner time.'

Barry pointed at Norbert, who was throwing a branch on to the bonfire.

'Ask him, monkey-features. We spent twenty minutes trying to drag him off a tree!'

The branch rolled back and nearly hit Norbert in the face. He had another go, but it fell down again. While he was doing this, Trevor crept up behind him. He grinned at Tony, Barry and me and took a jumping jack out of his pocket. He lit it, threw it down by Norbert's feet and ran over to us. Norbert threw the branch up again and this time it stayed on top, and just as he was turning round with a cheer, the jumping jack went off and scared the living daylights out of him. We all laughed like anything, but Norbert didn't think it was funny.

'Who did that? I bet it was you.'

He ran towards me.

Trevor pulled another jumping jack out of his pocket and waved it at Norbert. Norbert went for him, but Trevor was too quick. Norbert chased after him and got him in a stranglehold. Somehow. Trevor got out of it.

'Blooming heck, Norbert, your hands don't half pong. What've you been up to?'

Barry and me laughed our heads off. So did Tony when we told him. Trevor didn't. He ran off home to have a wash. It was dinner time by now, so we all decided to go home. Except Norbert. He never goes home on a Saturday. His mum just gives him some money for his dinner, and he stays out all day. I wouldn't like it if my mum did that. I went over to get my bike.

'See you, Norbert.'

Norbert had gone back to throwing branches on to the fire.

'Yeah, maybe see you later.'

'Yeah, maybe.'

I started walking with Tony and Barry, pushing my bike, but then I decided to cycle on ahead.

'I'd better get going. My mum'll be getting fish and chips.'

We always have fish and chips on a Saturday. I pedalled off just as Barry called after me.

'We'll come round after, have a look at your fireworks.'

Oh blimey! I braked.

'Oh, I've just remembered, I've got to go to my Auntie Doreen's with my mum. My Auntie Doreen is doing her hair. I've just remembered.'

That wasn't a complete lie. My mum was going to my Auntie Doreen's to have her hair done, but I didn't have to go with her. Ooh, why had I opened my big mouth earlier on? They're bound to find out my mum hadn't bought me any fireworks, especially when I don't turn up for the bonfire on Monday. Why was I the only one not to have my own fireworks?

I took a short cut through the park. You're not supposed to cycle in the park but it was a lot quicker. Anyway, there was hardly anybody about and the Park Ranger was most likely having his dinner. As I was going past the swings and slides, I saw this ginger-headed lad sitting on the kiddies' roundabout. It was going round very slowly, and he had a brown paper bag on his lap. Nobody else was about.

'Hey, you're not supposed to ride bikes in the park.'

He had a blooming cheek, because children over twelve aren't allowed on the swings and roundabouts, and this lad looked about fourteen.

'Well, you're not supposed to ride on the roundabouts if you're over twelve.'

He pushed himself round a bit faster with his foot.

'I know.'

He was a funny-looking kid. I didn't know him, but I'd seen him around a few times. He was always on his own. I think he went to St Matthew's. He held up the paper bag.

'Do you want to see summat?'

I wondered what he'd got in it.

'No, I'm late for my dinner.'

He stopped the roundabout with his foot.

'I've got some fireworks in this bag.'

I got off my bike, and wheeled it over. He did have fireworks in his bag. Tons of them. Bangers, volcanoes, silver cascades, dive-bombers, jumping jacks, flowerpots - everything. Every firework you'd ever seen.

'Where did you get them?'

He looked at me.

'From a shop. Do you want to buy 'em?'

'I haven't got any money.'

That's when I thought of it. I must've been mad. I was mad.

'I'll swop my bike for them.'

He got off the roundabout.

'All right.'

He held out the paper bag and I took it, and he took my bike and cycled off.

I must've been off my head. I ran home clutching my paper bag. I went in the back way, and hid my fireworks in the outhouse, behind the dustbin. I didn't enjoy my fish and chips at all. I kept thinking about my stupid swop. How could I have been so daft? I still had to go to the firework display at the Children's Hospital with my mum.

After dinner, my mum asked me if I wanted to go with her to my Auntie Doreen's.

'No, Mum, I said I might meet Tony and Barry.'

What I thought I'd do was go back to the park and try to find that lad and ask him to swop back. I mean, it wasn't a fair swop, was it?

'All right then love, but if you go anywhere on your bikes, be careful.'

I felt sick.

After my mum had gone, I went outside and got the bag of fireworks. I was looking at them in the front room when the doorbell rang. It couldn't have been my mum because she's got a key, but I put the fireworks in a cupboard just in case and went to answer it. Norbert, Barry and Tony were standing there. Barry looked at the others, then looked at me with a kind of smile.

'We saw your mum going up Deardon Street. She said you were at home.'

I didn't say anything. I just looked at them. Norbert sniffed.

'Yeah. So we thought we'd come and look at your fireworks.'

Norbert grinned his stupid grin. I could've hit him, but I didn't have to.

'You don't believe I've got any fireworks, do you?'

Tony and Barry didn't say anything. Norbert did.

'No!'

'I'll show you.'

I took them into the front room, and got the bag of fireworks out of the cupboard. I put them on the carpet, and we all kneeled round to have a look. They were really impressed, especially Norbert.

'Blooming hummer, did your mum buy you all these?'

'Course. I told you.'

Norbert kept picking one up after the other.

'But there's everything. Look at these dive-bombers. And look at the size of these rockets!'

Tony picked up an electric storm.

'These are great. They go on for ages.'

The three of them kept going through all the fireworks. They just couldn't believe it. I felt really chuffed.

'I'd better put them away now.'

Norbert had taken out a sparkler.

'I've never seen sparklers as big as these. Let's light one.'

'No, I'm putting them away now.'

I wanted to get rid of Barry, Tony and Norbert, and see if I could find that lad in the park. I'd proved I'd got my own fireworks now. I'd make up some excuse for not coming to the bonfire on Monday, but none of them could say I hadn't been given my own fireworks. None of them could say that, now.

'Go on, light a sparkler, just one. They're quite safe.'

Well, what harm would it do? Just one sparkler. I got the matches from the mantelpiece, and Norbert held it while I lit it. When it got going, I took hold of it, and we all sat round in a circle and watched it sparkle away. Suddenly, Tony screamed.

I looked down and saw lots of bright colours. For a split second I couldn't move. I was paralysed.

Suddenly, fireworks were flying everywhere. Bangers went off, rockets were flying. Sparks were shooting up to the ceiling. It was terrifying. Norbert hid behind the sofa, and Tony stood by the door, while Barry and me tried to put out the fireworks by stamping on them. I could hear Tony shouting, asking if he should fetch my mum.

'Yeah, get her, get her, she's at my Auntie Doreen's, get her!'

I don't know how long it took us, it could have been half an hour, it could have been five minutes, but somehow Barry and me managed to put all the fireworks out. The room was full of smoke, and we were coughing and choking like anything, and I couldn't stop myself from shaking, and even though I was sweating, I felt really cold.

As the smoke cleared, I saw my mum standing by the door, her hair wringing wet, and all I remember thinking was that I wouldn't need an excuse for not going to the bonfire on Monday.

She Was Afraid of Upstairs

by Joan Aiken

My cousin Tessie, that was. Bright as a button, she was, good as gold, neat as ninepence. And clever, too. Read anything she would time she were five. Papers, letters, library books, all manner of print. Delicate little thing, peaky, not pretty at all, but, even when she was a liddle un, she had a way of putting things into words that'd surprise you. 'Look at the sun a-setting, Ma,' she'd say. 'He's wrapping his hair all over his face.' Of the old postman, Jumper, on his red bike, she said he was bringing news from Otherwhere. And a bit of Demarara on a lettuce leaf - that was her favourite treat - a sugarleaf, she called it. 'But I haven't been good enough for a sugarleaf today,' she'd say. 'Have I, Ma?'

Good she mainly was, though, like I said, not a bit of harm in her.

But upstairs she would not go.

Been like that from a tiny baby, she had, just as soon as she could notice anything. When my Aunt Sarah would try to carry her up, she'd shriek and carry on, the way you'd think she was being taken to the slaughterhouse. At first they thought it was on account she didn't want to go to bed, maybe afraid of the dark, but that weren't it at all. For she'd settle to bed anywhere they put her, in the back kitchen, the broom closet under the stairs, in the lean-to with the copper, even in the coalshed, where my Uncle Fred once, in a temper, put her cradle. 'Let her lie there,' he said, 'if she won't sleep up in the bedroom, let her lie there.'

And lie there she did, calm and peaceable, all the livelong night, and not a chirp out of her.

My Aunt Sarah was fair put about with this awkward way of Tessie's, for they'd only the one downstairs room, and, evenings, you want the kids out of the way. One that won't go upstairs at night is a fair old problem. But, when Tessie was three, Uncle Fred and Aunt Sarah moved to Birmingham, where they had a back kitchen and a little bit of garden, and in the garden my Uncle Fred built Tessie a tiny cabin, not much bigger than a packing-case it wasn't, by the back kitchen wall, and there she had her cot, and there she slept, come rain, come snow.

Would she go upstairs in the day?

Not if she could help it.

'Run up, Tessie, and fetch me my scissors - or a clean towel - or the hair brush - or the bottle of camomile,' Aunt Sarah might say, when Tessie was big enough to walk and to run errands. Right away, her lip would start to quiver and that frantic look would come in her eye. But my Aunt Sarah was not a one to trifle with. She'd lost the big battle, over where Tessie was to sleep. She wasn't going to have any nonsense in small ways. Upstairs that child would have to go, whether she liked it or not. And upstairs she went, with Aunt Sarah's eye on her, but you could hear, by the sound of her feet, that she was having to drag them, one after the other, they were so unwilling, it was like hauling rusty nails out of wood. And when she was upstairs, the timid tiptoeing, it was like some wild creature, a squirrel or a bird that has got in by mistake. She'd find the thing, whatever it was, that Aunt Sarah wanted, and then, my word, wouldn't she come dashing down again as if the Militia were after her, push the thing, whatever it might be, into her mum's hands, and then out into the garden to take in big gulps of the fresh air. Outside was where she liked best to be, she'd spend whole days in the garden, if Aunt Sarah let her. She had a little patch, where she grew lettuce and cress. Uncle Fred got the seeds for her, and then people used to give her bits of slips and flower-seeds. She had a real gift for getting things to grow. That garden was a pretty place, you couldn't see the ground for the greenstuff and flowers. Narcissus, bluebells, sweetpeas, marigolds.

Of course the neighbours used to come and shove their oar in. Neighbours always will. 'Have a child that won't go upstairs? I'd not allow it if she was mine,' said Mrs Oakley that lived over the way. 'It's fair daft if you ask me. I'd soon leather her out of it.' For in other people's houses Tessie was just the same - when she got old enough to be taken out to tea. Upstairs she would not go. Anything but that.

Of course they used to try and reason with her, when she was old enough to express herself.

'Why don't you go, Tessie? What's the matter with upstairs? There's nothing bad up there. Only the beds and the chests-of-drawers. What's wrong with that?'

And Aunt Sarah used to say, laughing, 'You're nearer to heaven up there.'

But no, Tessie'd say, 'It's bad, it's bad! Something bad is up there.' When she was very little she'd say, 'Darkwoods. Darkwoods,' and 'Grandfather Moon! I'm frightened, I'm frightened!' Funny thing that, because, of the old moon itself, a-sailing in the sky, she wasn't scared a bit, loved it dearly, and used to catch the silvery light in her hands, if she were out at night, and say it was like tinsel falling from the sky.

Aunt Sarah was worried what would happen when Tessie started school. Suppose the school had an upstairs classroom, then what? But Uncle Fred told her not to fuss herself, not to borrow trouble; very likely the child would have got over all her nonsense by the time she was of school age, as children mostly do.

A doctor got to hear of her notions, for Tessie had the diptheery, one time, quite bad, with a thing in her throat, and he had to come ever so many times.

'This isn't a proper place to have her,' he says, for her bed was in the kitchen - it was winter then, they couldn't except the doctor to go out to Tessie's little cubbyhole in the garden. So Aunt Sarah began to cry and carry on, and told him how it was.

'I'll soon make an end of that nonsense,' says he, 'for now she's ill she won't notice where she is. And then, when she's better, she'll wake up and find herself upstairs, and her phobia will be gone.' That's what he called it, a phobia. So he took Tessie out of her cot and carried her upstairs. And, my word, didn't she create! Shruk! You'd a thought she was being skinned alive. Heads was poking out of windows all down the street. He had to bring her down again fast. 'Well, she's got a good strength in her, she's not going to die of the diptheery, at all events,' says he, but he was very put out, you could see that. Doctors don't like to be crossed. 'You've got a wilful one there, Missus,' says he, and off he goes, in high dudgeon. But he must have told another doctor about Tessie's wilfulness, for a week or so later, along comes a Doctor Trossick, a mind doctor, one of them pussycologists, who wants to ask Tessie all manner of questions. Does she remember this, does she remember that, when she was a baby, and why won't she go upstairs, can't she tell him the reason, and what's all this about Grandfather Moon and Darkwoods? Also, what about when her Ma and Pa go upstairs, isn't she scared for them too?

'No, it's not dangerous for them,' says Tessie. 'Only for me.'

'But why is it dangerous for you, child? What do you think is going to happen?'

'Something dreadful! The worst possible thing!'

Dr Trossick made a whole lot of notes, asked Tessie to do all manner of tests on a paper he'd brought, and then he tried to make her go upstairs, persuading her to stand on the bottom step for a minute, and then on the next one, and the one after. But by the fourth step she'd come to trembling and shaking so bad, with the tears running down, that he hadn't the heart to force her any further.

So things stood, when Tessie was six or thereabouts. And then one day the news came: the whole street where they lived was going to be pulled down. Redevelopment. Rehousing. All the little two-up, two-downs were to go, and everybody was to be shifted to high-rise blocks. Aunt Sarah, Uncle Fred, and Tessie were offered a flat on the sixteenth floor of a block that was already built.

Aunt Sarah was that upset. She loved her little house. And as for Tessie - 'It'll kill her for sure,' Aunt Sarah said.

At that, Uncle Fred got riled. He was a slow man, but obstinate.

'We can't arrange our whole life to suit a child,' he said. 'We've been offered a Council flat - very good, we'll take it. The kid will have to learn she can't have her own way always. Besides,' he said, 'there's lifts in them blocks. Maybe when she finds she can go up in a lift, she won't take on as much as if it was only stairs. And maybe the sixteenth floor won't seem so bad as the first or second. After all, we'll all be on one level - there's no stairs in a flat.'

Well, Aunt Sarah saw the sense in that. And the only thing she could think of was to take Tessie to one of the high-rise blocks and see what she made of it. Her cousin Ada, that's my Mum, had already moved into one of the tower blocks, so Aunt Sarah took Tessie out in her pushchair one afternoon and fetched her over to see us.

All was fine to start with, the kid was looking about her, interested and not too bothered, till the pushchair was wheeled into the lift and the doors closed.

'What's this?' says Tessie then.

'It's a lift,' says Aunt Sarah, 'and we're going to see your Auntie Ada and Winnie and Dorrie.'

Well, when the lift started going up, Aunt Sarah told us, Tessie went white as a dishclout, and time it got up to the tenth, that was where we lived, she was flat on the floor. Fainted. A real bad faint it was, she didn't come out of it for ever so long, and Aunt Sarah was in a terrible way over it.

'What have I done, what have I done to her,' she kept saying.

We all helped her get Tessie home again. But after that the kid was very poorly. Brain fever, they'd have called it in the old days, Mum said. Tossing and turning, hot as fire, and delirious with it, wailing and calling out about Darkwoods and Grandfather Moon. For a long time they was too worried about her to make any plans at all, but when she began to mend, Aunt Sarah says to Uncle Fred:

'Now what are we going to do?'

Well, he was very put out, natural, but he took his name off the Council list and began to look for another job, somewhere else, where they could live on ground level. And at last he found work in a little seaside town, Topness, about a hundred miles off. Got a house and all, so they was set to move.

They didn't want to shift before Tessie was middling better, but the Council was pushing and pestering them to get out of their house, because the whole street was coming down; the other side had gone already, there was just a big huge stretch of grey rubble, as far as you could see, and half the houses on this side was gone too.

'What's happening?' Tessie kept saying when she looked out of the window. 'What's happening to our world?'

She was very pitiful about it.

'Are they going to do that with my garden too?' she'd say. 'All my sweetpeas and marigolds?'

'Don't you worry, dearie,' days Aunt Sarah. 'You can have a pretty garden where we're going.'

'And I won't have to sleep upstairs?'

'No, no, Dad'll fix you a cubbyhole, same as he has here.'

So they packed up all their bits and sticks and they started off. Sam Whitelaw lent them his grocery van for the move, and he drove it too.

It was a long drive - over a hundred miles, and most of it through wild, bare country. Tessie liked it all right at first, she stared at the green fields and the sheep, she sat on Aunt Sarah's lap and looked out of the window, but after a few hours, when they were on the moor, she began to get very poorly, her head was as hot as fire, and her hands too. She didn't complain, but she began to whimper with pain and weakness, big tears rolled down, and Aunt Sarah was bothered to death about her.

'The child wasn't well enough to shift yet. She ought to be in a bed. What'll we do?'

'We're only halfway, if that,' says Mr Whitelaw. 'D'you want to stop somewhere, Missus?'

The worst of it was, there weren't any houses round there - not a building to be seen for miles and miles.

On they went, and now Tessie was throwing herself from side to side, delirious again, and crying fit to break her mother's heart.

At last, ahead of them - it was glimmery by then, after sunset of a wintry day - they saw a light, and came to a little old house, all by itself, set a piece back off the road against a wooded scarp of hill.

'Should we stop here and see if the folk will help us?' suggested Mr Whitelaw, and Aunt Sarah says, 'Oh, yes. Yes! Maybe they have a phone and can send for a doctor. Oh I'm worried to death,' she says. 'It was wicked to move the child so soon.'

The two men went and tapped at the door and somebody opened it. Uncle Fred explained about the sick child, and the owner of the house - an old, white-haired fellow, Aunt Sarah said he was - told them, 'I don't have a phone, look'ee, I live here all on my own. But you're kindly welcome to come in and put the poor little mawther in my bed.'

So they all carried Tessie in among them - by that time she was hardly sensible. My poor aunt gave a gasp when she stepped inside, for the house was really naught but a barn or shippen, with a floor of beaten earth and some farm stuff, tumbrils and carts and piles of turnips.

'Up here,' says the old man, and shows them a flight of stone steps by the wall.

Well, there was nothing for it; up they had to go.

Above was decent enough, though. The old fellow had two rooms, fitted up as bedroom and kitchen, with an iron cooking-stove, curtains at the windows, and a bed covered with old blankets, all felted up. Tessie was almost too ill to notice where she'd got to. They put her on the bed, and the old man went to put on a kettle - Aunt Sarah thought the child should have a hot drink.

Uncle Fred and Mr Whitelaw said they'd drive on in the van and fetch a doctor, if the old man could tell them where to find one.

'Surely,' says he, 'there's a doctor in the village - Wootten-under-Edge, five miles along. Dr Hastie - he's a real good un, he'll come fast enough.'

'Where is this place?' says Uncle Fred. 'Where should we tell him to come?'

'He'll know where it is,' says the old man. 'Tell him Darkwoods Farm.'

Off they went, and the old man came back to where Aunt Sarah was trying to make poor Tessie comfortable. The child was tossing and fretting, whimpering and crying that she felt so ill, her head felt so bad!

'She'll take a cup of my tansy tea. That'll soothe her,' said the old man, and he went to his kitchen and brewed up some green drink in an old blue-and-white jug.

'Here, Missus,' said he, coming back. 'Try her with a little of this.'

A sip or two did seem to soothe poor Tessie, brung her to herself a bit, and for the first time she opened her eyes and took a look at the old man.

'Where is this place?' she asked. She was so weak, her voice was no more than a thread.

'Why, you're in my house,' said the old man. 'And very welcome you are, my dear!'

'And who are you?' she asked next.

'Why, lovey, I'm old Tom Moon the shepherd - old Grandfather Moon. I lay you never expected you'd be sleeping in the moon's house tonight!'

But at that, Tessie gave one screech, and fainted dead away.

Well, poor Aunt Sarah was that upset, with trying to bring Tessie round, but she tried to explain to Mr Moon about Tessie's trouble, and all her fears, and the cause of her sickness.

He listened, quiet and thinking, taking it all in.

Then he went and sat down by Tessie's bed, gripping hold of her hand.

She was just coming round by then, she looked at him

with big eyes full of fright, as Aunt Sarah kneeled down by her other side.

'Now, my dearie,' said Mr Moon. 'You know I'm a shepherd, I never hurt a sheep or a lamb in my life. My job is to look after 'em, see? And I'm certainly not a-going to hurt you. So don't you be frit now - there's nothing to be frightened of. Not from old Grandfather Moon.'

But he could see that she was trembling all over.

'You've been scared all your life, haven't you, child?' said he gently, and she nodded, Yes.

He studied her then, very close, looked into her eyes, felt her head, and held her hands.

And he said, 'Now, my dearie, I'm not going to tell ye no lies. I've never told a lie yet - you can't be lying to sheep or lambs. Do ye believe that I'm your friend and wish you well?'

Again she gave a nod, even weaker.

He said, 'Then, Tessie my dear, I have to tell you that you're a-going to die. And that's what's been scaring you all along. But you were wrong to be in such a fret over it, lovey, for there's naught to be scared of. There'll be no hurt, there'll be no pain, it be just like stepping through a door. And I should know,' he said, 'for I've seen a many, many sheep and lambs taken off by weakness or the cold. It's no more than going to sleep in one life and waking up in another. Now do ye believe me, Tessie?'

Yes, she nodded, with just a hint of a smile, and she turned her eyes to Aunt Sarah, on the other side of the bed.

And with that, she took and died.

The Turning Tide

by David Harmer

Liz Campbell pushed away the long dark hair from her face and shivered. The East Coast haze was beginning to turn cold as icy rain rattled against her cagoule. Reluctantly the straggle of children sitting on rocks piled near the beach put down their packed lunches and began to pull waterproof clothing from their bags and rucksacks.

Liz looked out to sea. A giant smudge, grey and smokey, was beginning to scud over the waves towards them. She sighed. It was a pity. This far out from the town they were completely exposed to the weather. Of course all the children were well protected against its attacks but it had been such a lovely warm morning that it was a shame things were changing to rapidly for the worse. Perhaps it would settle later. Conditions on the Yorkshire coast were very changeable in June.

She walked over to a group of youngsters who were snuggling down in their cagoules to finish their lunch in the lee of some boulders. She would have to keep a careful eye on some of these. They were only nine, after all. Norman Armstrong's fourth years might be able to brave a stiff shower gusting in from the North Sea but some of these younger ones would feel it keenly.

'You lot OK down there?' she asked.

'Yes Mrs Campbell. Its brill,' said Mandy Ricks.

'I've got sand in my sandwiches,' giggled Adam Clayton, 'great big lumps of it.'

Liz smiled and moved towards the next group. They were mainly fourth years and were surrounding the kneeling figure of Norman Armstrong, Liz's colleague from York Street school. He was bending over something that he seemed to have planted in the sand. The children were trying to shield him from the wind and judging from his exasperated comments they weren't succeeding. Of course, Liz reflected, he was always losing his temper about something, but even she couldn't work out what it might be this time. Not on a beach.

She grinned to herself, then regained her straight face

when she realised that Mr Khan was part of the crowd surrounding Norman. Mr Khan had a girl in Liz's class and a son in Norman's. It wouldn't do really for a parent to see her laughing at yet another of Norman's struggles.

Norman was wrapped in a vast blue waterproof suit with the legs of his habitual track suit poking out at the ankles. He was obviously finding his bulky clothing a hindrance and whatever it was that he was trying to stand up kept falling over.

'Everything all right there, Mr Armstrong?' Liz asked.

'What? Eh? Oh, it's you Mrs Campbell.' A large face, flushed and sweating above a bright red moustache, shot up from among the knees and elbows of the surrounding group. 'No, not really. This thing keeps going wrong.'

'What is it exactly?'

'What is it? Isn't it obvious?' She could see now, as he stood up, that he was caked in sand. Rain continued to mingle with beads of sweat down his purple cheeks and he was very out of breath. 'It's my weather vane. My weather vane won't function.'

'Oh.' Liz had to turn quickly, choking back her laughter. She stared with fixed determination at a large bird that shot, straighter than her expression, flat over the grey sea like a long black arrow.

'It's a cormorant Mrs Campbell,' said Mark Doaks standing right beside her.

'Are cormorants funny, Mrs Campbell?' asked a girl standing beside Mark. 'I mean, like penguins?'

'No, Jenny' replied Liz carefully, 'I just ...'

'Look.' Mr Armstrong burst through his protective cocoon of helpers and waved something under Liz's nose. 'See? Useless. Broken. No good at all.'

He had in his hand a washing-up liquid bottle with the top third cut away. In his other hand he held a complicated wooden structure topped by a cardboard propellor and a rod with a paper N stuck on one end.

'Right. Two sections. Won't fit. Keeps blowing over.

Worked fine in class, didn't it Jenny?'

'Yes Mr Armstrong.'

Liz turned to her colleague. 'That's quite a gadget, Mr Armstrong. What should it do?'

'Isn't it obvious? Set it down on the sand and it will show which way the wind is blowing.'

'Couldn't you just wet your thumb and stick it in the air?'

'Mrs Campbell! Have you seriously thought out the CDT implications of today's visit? I wonder if you have?'

'Yes,' she replied calmly, 'of course I have.'

'Ah well, er, you see, well. Hey!' Suddenly Mr Armstrong shot off in alarm as a gust of wind jerked the wooden part of his device out of his hand and sent it skating over a section of shingle and sand.

Liz was not the only one who could not prevent equally powerful gusts of laughter rushing out as Norman's blue bulk billowed over the beach in a futile attempt to prevent the weather vane ending up in the sea. A helpful wave brought the contraption within paddling distance. Rolling up his leggings and track suit, Norman pulled off his already soaking trainers and stomped into the freezing water, his thin white legs gleaming through the waves.

'Don't paddle too far, Mr Armstrong' Jenny called out. 'Its deep out there!' Her comment was followed by ragged applause as Norman retrieved his invention.

'Awful weather, Mrs Rogers' commented Liz as she sat next to one of the mothers who had joined them that day.

'Oh yes. It is. Set for the day of course. Still, what can you expect? Sandthorpe. Unpredictable is this place, even in June.'

Liz munched her sandwiches and stared at the white hotels and sloping rooftops that blurred in the hazy distance as the sweep of the bay became engulfed in mist and drizzle. She began to mull over the morning's activity. It had gone very well. The children had written and measured and drawn. They had investigated a variety of rock pools without disturbing the inhabitants too much. They had watched for different birds, caught sight of distant shipping and had seen at close quarters two men row a crabbing boat over the then flat surface of Sandthorpe Bay. The men had rowed so far, then carefully offloaded their lines of pots, all roped together with an orange marker buoy for each one. It had been a fascinating morning. Norman, of course, had stamped and grunted all over the place like a small, blue, bad-tempered airship, generally getting in everybody's way, but a lot of useful and productive work had been done. Now it seemed that this squall could settle into a steady downpour and ruin the afternoon.

Several metres away from where Liz was sitting, Jenny Cartwright and Mark Doakes were with a group of friends finishing off their lunch.

'Packed lunch?' Mark was sceptical. 'You look as if you've packed the rations for an entire army, Javed.'

'Well,' Javed Khan grinned 'I have to keep my strength up. After all, Barmy Army needs my help with that weather vane.'

'Yes,' said Mark, 'what is that thing exactly? What's it supposed to do?'

'It tells you which way the wind is blowing' explained Javed.

'Who wants to know that?' asked Mark.

Javed shrugged 'I don't know,' he said 'I didn't make the stupid thing.'

Mark was surprised. 'Didn't you? I thought you, John and Gita built it last week in school.'

'No, we began it but then Barmy Army began to interfere. Said we were doing it wrong. In the end he did it all. All it does now is fall over.'

'Mrs Campbell was laughing like mad,' said Jenny.

'I'm not surprised,' said Javed gloomily, 'it's rubbish.'

'This weather's getting worse,' said Mark, 'we'll never get out on the Ridge now.'

Sandthorpe Ridge was a huge shelf of rock that jutted out into the sea in a great raft. When the tide was right it was possible to walk along it in complete safety and yet be surrounded by deep, foaming ocean. Liz had checked everything thoroughly with the Coastguards and knew that if she got onto the Ridge by two o'clock she would have an hour before she needed to turn back. Even then she had been assured that there was a good safety margin before the incoming tide would flood the width of the bay. However, the present conditions seemed to be spoiling any chance of even beginning the expedition.

'Nonsense!' growled Mr Armstrong, swigging back his coffee. 'We'll get out there all right. Bit risky for the tiny tots, I suppose, but my fourth years will cope. They are ...'

'If it is all the same with you' Mr Khan's quiet voice interrupted the assertive flow, 'my Javed will not be with you in this venture until the rain stops. Far too dangerous you know.'

Armstrong paused. 'Yes well, of course. Goes without saying, Mr Khan. Yes. Wait until the rain stops.'

'Oh, it won't do that, love,' said Mrs Rogers with a smile, 'not now. Set in for the day, this has.'

But she was wrong. As lunchtime passed and moved towards two o'clock a watery sun wobbled out from behind a thick sludge of cloud and pushed a few feeble rays towards the beach. Then the wind suddenly dropped and the rain petered out all together. Encouraged by this quick change of mood the sun got less wobbly until it was strong enough to try to shine properly. Half an hour later the whole school party was able to walk to where the Ridge joined the beach and began to reach out like an arm pointing the way to Holland.

All the children were excited by the thought of walking onto the Ridge, but Liz knew that her timing had been seriously delayed by the weather.

'Look, Norman,' she said 'it's 2.30 now. We'll go out a little way but we must turn back at three. OK?'

'I suppose so,' he agreed. 'If we must.'

The school party gathered around Liz and she quickly

allocated each of the adults a group of five children. Cautiously she began to lead the way over the first few rocks that lay at the entrance to the Ridge.

The stone, eroded and worn into countless whorls and patterns, was slippery but with care, easily negotiated. The whole platform was the width of about two soccer pitches and there was no danger at all as long as everybody stuck to the middle of the Ridge. On either side of them the sea thundered and rocketed, filling the air with spray. The wind freshened and the sun grew stronger.

'Look, Mrs Campbell,' cried Adam Clayton, 'look at the gulls.'

In front of them - Liz couldn't say exactly how far because distances were deceptive - a grey cloud of gulls hung over the edge of the Ridge. The whole structure seemed to narrow quite dramatically at that point and sea water smashed violently against both sides, flinging up huge curtains of spray. As the water hurtled upwards, so the entire flock of gulls rose and then subsided like a vast wave.

'What are they doing Mrs Campbell?' asked Mandy. 'Why are they bouncing up and down like yo-yos?'

'I don't know, really,' replied the teacher 'it's very odd isn't it? Perhaps the sea washes up scraps for them to eat, dead fish, that sort of thing. They're scavengers, you know, these gulls, like vultures.'

'I thought vultures were wrinkled and bald' said Adam.

'No, that's your dad' giggled Mandy.

The groups of children were now approaching the gulls. The air was thick with bird cries and wet with a shower of sea water. A fine crust of salt covered everybody's face and hands and their cagoules were streaming. The wind grew stronger still.

'It's time to turn back.' Liz had to shout now, her words lost in the crash of the waves and the force of the wind. 'Time to turn back!'

The parents leading the other groups waved. They had heard her. She could see them begin to turn their parties around.

'Do we have to go, Mrs Campbell?' groaned Mandy. 'It's brill here.'

'Yes we do, now come on.' She looked at her watch. It was 2.50. Despite the wild appearance of the sea she was well within her safety limit. Everybody would have plenty of time to reach the shore. She began to count heads. It was then, as she saw Mr Pound's group actually reach the safety of the beach, that she realised Norman was not in front of her.

He was behind her, still on the Ridge, near the gulls. Standing next to the familiar blue balloon-like figure were several smaller figures all staring out to sea.

'Norman!' she shouted. 'Mr Armstrong! The tide is beginning to turn! Come back!' It was useless. Her voice was caught by the wind and tossed back towards the cliffs like driftwood on the running tide.

Norman could see Liz fairly clearly through the spray. He could see that all the other groups, including hers, had now reached the shoreline and that his group were the last to turn back. He glanced at his watch, a Diver's Digital Special. It had cost him quite a lot of money. It was shockproof, waterproof and antimagnetic. It had a built-in stop watch and a calendar function as well as a loud alarm. It was in many ways a superb piece of equipment. The only trouble was that at this precise moment it said 1.45, which meant that it was broken.

Unlike his watch, Mr Armstrong was not shock-proof. He felt his stomach lurch and fall like the sea that crashed around him.

'Oh no!' he cried. 'No. Can't be. Batteries. A malfunction. Quick, what time is it?'

'It's ten past three, Mr Armstrong,' said Mark. 'Why?'

'The tide. It's on the turn. Quick. Go. My watch - no good. Go. Go.'

He began to take the children back. His urgency grew as he imagined a huge sweep of water embracing the entire bay, accelerating as it drew nearer and crashing over all of them.

In his haste he suddenly slipped on the greasy surface of a smooth patch of rock. With a yell he flung up his arms and tumbled like a goal keeper failing to stop a penalty.

'My ankle' he yelled. 'My ankle!'

The children stopped. They could see him stretched out on the wet rocks, trying to struggle to his feet, only to moan loudly with pain and slump to his knees.

The wind blew an icy blast into their faces as they froze with fear, stuck to the rocks like limpets. A minute before they had felt so secure, surrounded by a storming sea but actually completely safe in the centre of the Ridge. Now a panic as icy as the tide flooded through them.

'Help. Get some help. Can't walk. The tide. Get a move on!' Mr Armstrong's voice, as irritable as ever, for once acted positively. Jenny broke from the numbing hold of that first shock.

'Come on,' she said, 'let's get organised. Chris, me and Tony - we'll try to get Mr Armstrong up and moving as best we can. You two, you run back to Mrs Campbell as quickly as possible. She'll know what to do.'

The two runners scrambled away immediately and the remaining three bent down beside Mr Armstrong who was, once again, trying to get to his feet. He gritted his teeth and spoke.

'Now look here, the ankle's gone, OK? You have to bear my weight.' He paused, 'Come on then. Get at it.'

The children knelt down beside his crouching figure and somehow struggled under his shoulders. Jenny felt the wet stickiness of the Ridge under the palms of her hand. It felt salty and tough, like the hide of some enormous, stony monster. Bringing up his good foot so that he was resting on one knee, Mr Armstrong pushed himself upwards. At the same moment the children rose and took most of his weight on their backs. They staggered forward, swayed and nearly fell. Mr Armstrong yelled and the children stiffened their legs to take the strain even more. Somehow they all managed to keep their balance. Then, like some huge, wounded crab, they began to drag themselves forward towards the beach.

Twice they nearly slipped and once Mr Armstrong shouted out as his swollen foot briefly wedged against a stone. They did make progress but all the time felt a giant clock ticking away behind them.

Jenny scarcely dared to look as she imagined water beginning to cover the far rim of the Ridge. It wouldn't be long, she knew, before it would be lapping at her feet.

The moment Liz got her party to the beach Mr Khan pointed to a spot behind her. Turning, she saw Simon Giltrap and Amanda Jacobs slithering over the Ridge. Behind them she saw the rescue party stumbling all too slowly towards safety.

'Mr Khan, can you help me here please?'

Briskly Liz organised matters on the shore and the parents began to walk the children back to the sea-front carpark where the coach was waiting for them. She then followed the purposeful figure of Mr Khan who was already striding out towards the injured teacher.

Jenny had to stop. Tide or no tide, her back was hurting and her cagoule ran with sweat. She dared herself a look behind. Already the furthest tip of the Ridge was invisible. Soon the whole flood would pour down on them and although she could see the cliff bottom quite plainly, at the speed they were making it seemed a long way away.

Then it registered with her that Liz and Mr Khan were nearly with them. 'Mr Armstrong' she said. 'Look. Here comes the cavalry.'

Liz saw Norman scowl, with either pain or annoyance. Probably both. She spoke brightly with a smile she didn't feel. 'You'll all be swimming back to the bus at this rate. Let's speed it up a bit, shall we?'

With the help of Mr Khan's broad shoulders the rescue operation accelerated noticably. When Jenny looked round this time she gasped. The spot just beyond where the gulls had gathered had gone. There was only sea across the bay's width. Most of the Ridge had vanished.

'Hurry up,' grunted Liz, 'the tide ...'

'Mrs Campbell,' Mr Khan spoke firmly 'it is quite all right. We are nearly there. We shall not drown.'

For all that, it was a difficult journey. The seaweed strung out over the rocks seemed to jam their feet into salty green webs that popped and cracked as they shuffled through. With each step, Norman seemed to grow heavier and the three children were obviously very tired. However, as they neared the margin of beach that joined the Ridge to the base of the cliffs, the coach driver and two local lobster men were there to help drag the exhausted Mr Armstrong those final, vital metres.

In fact it wasn't long before everybody was back on the bus and drinking hot coffee. Jenny looked back at where they had so recently been. It was as though the Ridge were some huge geological fantasy, a dream that had never existed. All she could see was a tiny strip of land and then a wide sweep of sea curling up at the cliff's edge.

'You all did well, very well.' It was Liz, standing in the aisle of the bus talking to the six children who had so nearly been trapped. 'And you too, Mr Khan, thank you very, very much.'

He grinned, 'Oh,' he said, 'it was nothing, really ...'

Her relief and heartfelt thanks were interrupted by a sudden roar from Mr Armstrong at the back of the coach where he was sitting, his bad ankle stretched out along the seat. She raced up the bus towards him.

'Norman, what is it? Are you all right?'

He looked up. Back there on the beach there had been a brief moment of real thanks, a fleeting apology, a slight smile. Now that was all gone. He glowered at her.

'What's wrong? You ask me that? I'll tell what's wrong. My model. My weather vane. You've left it on the beach.'

'I have? Me?'

'Well, I was hardly in a position to retrieve it, was I? And now it's missing. That's your responsibility Liz. I can tell you, I am most disappointed.'

Just as Liz was about to allow her exasperation at his ingratitude to explode, Javed Khan suddenly appeared.

'Look, Mr Armstrong. I have the weather vane. See?'

The boy held up the device for Mr Armstrong's inspection. It looked much as it did before except that Javed had managed to fix the two parts together. There was a chance the thing might actually work.

'Good' said Norman. 'Now Mrs Campbell, watch this. I think you'll find it instructive.' He leaned forward and blew vigorously into the cardboard sails.

For a moment the rod with the N on it swung in response. Everybody on the bus was now craning their necks to get a view and they all fell silent, eyes fixed on the model. With a triumphant smirk, Norman blew on it again.

The minute this second delivery of moving air caught the cardboard sails, they reacted a little differently. Instead of spinning round and moving the rod, they wobbled, teetered and began to fall. In a wild attempt to save them, Norman snatched the device from Javed Khan and succeeded in catching it with his finger. The whole thing catapulted into the air and over the backs of several seats to the enormous delight of the onlooking children.

It eventually landed at the feet of Adam Clayton.

'Mrs Campbell,' he called up the coach 'this rocket thing's all smashed up.'

Liz, not for the first time that day, had to look very quickly away from Norman Armstrong and once again found herself gazing out to sea, this time through the bus window. She, like Jenny beside her, saw no Ridge but a flat expanse of water, calmer now, with the sun bravely shining and the waves gently rolling up at the cliff's foot. A short dark line stabbed across her view. As she heard Norman fuming and muttering behind her she had to stare at it very hard.

'I think its another cormorant, Mrs Campbell' smiled Jenny, 'don't you?'

Butch!

by Christine Bentley

When Dad brought the dog home I couldn't believe it, I just couldn't believe it.

I had always wanted a dog - a silky red-haired setter with a soft brown eyes or a cuddly corgi or a cute little chihuahua or a soft golden labrador or a frisky black and white collie or a white woolly poodle. I would have settled for almost any kind of dog. But I certainly did not want a dog like Butch.

'Well, here we are,' said Dad sheepishly as he tried to pull this fat snarling creature through the door. Eventually he managed to get the brute inside and it was then that I stared in disbelief.

There stood Butch, a big, ugly, barrel-bodied, bow-legged bull terrier with square pinky-white jowls and pale unfriendly eyes. The monster growled as it caught sight of me, showed a set of sharp teeth like tank traps and stuck its fat tail in the air.

'I know what you're thinking, Christine,' said Dad quickly. 'I know it's not what you ...' His voice tailed off.

'Dad, it's horrible!' I cried.

We had inherited Butch. My father's uncle, who had recently died, had left us, along with his medals, an assortment of glass and china, and a grandfather clock, his 'true and faithful companion' - Butch. The dog had been with a neighbour of Uncle Alex's since the old man's death. It was with a great sense of relief that the poor neighbour was relieved of the creature.

'He's a very grumpy dog,' she told Dad. 'Very particular about his food, and he tends to bite anything that moves.'

'I'm sure he's a very friendly dog, deep down,' said Dad unconvincingly. 'We'll soon get to like him.'

But Butch wasn't and we didn't. He turned out to be bad-tempered and moody and one hour after his arrival the entire bird population of the street migrated and next door's cat made itself scarce. The little hedgehog which had scampered across the lawn every night for his bowl of milk returned to hibernation.

Butch soon made himself at home. Each morning he would sit in the middle of the garden path sunning himself and watching for any movement. Then people stopped calling. Gillian, my best friend, informed me that she would meet me at school in future, the milkman left the deliveries at the gate, the postman posted our letters next door and asked for them to be passed on and the newspaper boy threw the paper over the hedge.

Then one morning the inevitable happened. Sooner or later we knew he would kill something. I had just finished my breakfast when Butch wandered into the kitchen with a black and white rabbit wedge in his jaws.

'Dad! Dad!' I screamed. 'Come quickly.'

Dad bounded down the stairs and rushed into the kitchen.

'Look!' I cried. 'It's got a rabbit!'

'Oh my goodness!' gasped Dad. He grabbed Butch by his collar. 'Drop!' he commanded. 'Drop!'

Butch looked up with the grey, watery, button eyes of a shark and tightened his grip on the rabbit.

'I said drop it!' shrieked Dad, his voice two octaves higher by this time. 'This instant!'

Butch made a rumbling noise like a distant train.

'Do you hear me, you ... you nasty, vicious, savage cur!'

Butch blinked, then flopped down on the carpet still gripping his victim.

Dad attempted everything: trying to prize open the jaws with a brush, tapping him on the head, dangling a morsel of juicy meat in front of his nose, nipping his nose to cut off his air, but nothing worked.

'There's nothing for it,' said Dad suddenly. 'We'll have to take it to the vet's.'

'It's the wolfish ancestry,' explained the vet as he surveyed Butch as he stood bow-legged and brazen on his examination table. 'It's over ten thousand years, you know, since dogs were first domesticated but they still retain their wild instincts. We have modified a great many of their wild traits, of course, but all dogs still have that basic urge to kill. Even the most endearing of puppies is quite capable of savagery.'

'Much as I would like a potted history of the canine world,' interrupted Dad getting irritated, 'I do want to know what you can do about the rabbit.'

'Not much, I'm afraid. It's dead,' replied the vet flatly. 'It's been dead for hours. As soon as the dog grabbed it, the rabbit had no chance, no chance at all. Bull terriers have jaws like iron clamps. The rabbit's backbone would have been cracked like a nut.'

'I know it's dead,' said Dad. 'I guessed it was dead as soon as I saw it. What are you going to do about it?'

'Well I can't revive it, if that's what you're thinking.'

'I don't expect you to work miracles, Mr Fox,' said Dad. 'I just want the rabbit removing. The dog can't go through the rest of its life with a dead rabbit stuffed in its mouth!'

The vet agreed. He stroked Butch on the fat, round head and then tickled him behind the ears.

'He seems to like that,' said the vet smiling.

Dad glowered.

A minute later Butch sort of yawned and the rabbit flopped out.

'There we are,' chortled the vet. 'You just have to know the right spot.' He picked up the rabbit and examined it. 'Oh, this creature has been dead for hours, in fact it's beginning to smell.'

Having settled what Dad thought to be an exorbitant bill for merely tickling a dog, we departed.

After some detective work on my part we discovered that the rabbit belonged to a little girl who lived at the end of the street.

'I don't know what I'm going to say,' sighed Dad. 'I bet that rabbit meant the world to her. She'll be heartbroken.'

'I'll come along to the house with you, Dad, and give you a bit of moral support,' I said.

The door was opened by a giant of a man with a great

hairy face and a tangle of curls.

'Yes?' he asked abruptly.

'Good evening,' started Dad. 'I've come ...'

'If it's double-glazing,' snapped the ogre, 'we don't want any, or anything else for that matter!'

'No it's not, er, double glazing ... it's about your little girl's rabbit.'

'What about it?' asked the man.

'It's dead,' said Dad quickly, thinking the best way forward was to be blunt and get it over with.

'Eh?'

'I said your little girl's rabbit's dead. I'm terribly sorry.'

'I know it's dead,' said the man. Then a curious look came over his face. 'It's, er, nice of you to call round. Like rabbits do you?'

'Well, I don't know many, really, but I felt I ought to, well, tell you that the rabbit's dead.' Dad shuffled uneasily on the doorstep.

'I know it's dead,' said the man. 'I buried it myself.'

'You buried it?' repeated Dad.

'Course I did, I buried it a couple of days ago,' said the man. 'I'll show you.'

So we followed the man down the path.

'It was an old rabbit and had been sickly for weeks. It wanted putting out of its misery, really, so when we found it dead in the hutch it was a blessing, really. My little Tracey's just about got over it.'

'Was it a black and white rabbit with a sort of patch over one eye?' asked Dad.

'That's it. His name was Springer. Won't be doing much springing now though.'

The man stopped at a spot underneath a willow tree. There was a hole in the soil. The man stared for a moment.

'I buried our Tracey's rabbit here,' he said with a puzzled expression. 'It looks as if something's dug it up. Probably that ginger tom from down the road.'

Dad looked at me and I at him. We both smiled.

'I can't see as how there's anything to laugh about.' said the man.

Just Like Nat Gonella

by Roger Burford-Mason

It was hardly worth opening on a Tuesday, Mr Sapper told himself. Tuesday is bad enough in an ordinary shop, but in a second-hand shop? Forget it.

He carried the stick-back chairs into the shop from the pavement, and returned for the lawnmower. When he went back out again there was a lad on a bike.

'Mind the window,' he said.

The boy nodded. It was a rough old bike, Sapper thought. Get about ten pounds for it at the most. The boy sat with his foot on the window ledge, looking intently at something in the window. Sapper picked up the box of paperback books and carried them in. When he went out again, the boy was gone. Sapper thought no more about it, and by three o'clock the shop was shut, the alarm was on and he was on his way home to see his beehives before tea. Most Tuesdays it was the same story.

Wednesday he had a good day. He sold the four stick-back chairs to a nice American officer from the local base, and made a few bob on them above what he'd been hoping for. Then in the afternoon a very airy-fairy couple had been in and bought some bric-a-brac. Turned out they were on the stage, buying stuff for props for a production of some Victorian play. Even gave him a couple of complimentary tickets. Nice to take the wife, Sapper thought, putting them carefully in his wallet, as if bending them might make them invalid. As he was locking up about five the boy appeared again out of nowhere. One minute he wasn't there as Sapper was getting stuff in off the pavement, then when he went back, there the lad was, propping up the windowsill and looking in the window at something.

Thursday it rained. He couldn't put his gear out on the pavement and as a consequence the shop was that cramped he wished he hadn't bothered to open at all. He got irritated because there wasn't anything useful he could do, only sit all day in his armchair reading the papers behind the chest of drawers that served him for a counter. Nobody came to the shop all morning. Who could blame them? You don't go out in the rain unless you've got to, and nobody's got to go to a junk shop so badly that they go while it's raining!

He had his lunch and saw out the dragging afternoon, always on the verge of closing and going home, but not quite getting round to it. He made a cup of tea at about four and as he was drinking it, he saw the boy arrive, prop himself up on the window ledge and stare in at something. Once he looked through the window and saw Mr Sapper looking at him, but he didn't register it by so much as a flicker, turning his attention again to whatever it was in the window he had come to look at. Sapper got angry at the boy then, and was about to go out and speak to him when the boy got off his bike abruptly and came into the shop. The little bell tinkled as the door opened.

'Propped your bike against the glass, did you?' Sapper said crossly.

The boy looked back in embarrassment at the bike leaning against the window and did not answer. Rainwater leaked out of his shoes and made a broadening patch where he was standing.

'I'm packing up in a minute,' Sapper said gruffly. 'So don't imagine you can come messing about in here to get out of the rain, wasting my time.'

The boy shifted uncomfortably.

'That trumpet,' he said with obvious effort. 'How much is it?'

Sapper followed the direction of his gesture.

'Is there a trumpet there?' he said. He knew there was, and was only being awkward because he'd had such a bad day.

'By the old cash register,' the boy said. 'In a black case.'

'Oh that trumpet,' Sapper said, playing for time. 'Fine instrument that. Boosey and Hawkes if my memory serves me right.'

The boy nodded like a wise little old man. Sapper noticed his clean but frayed shirt and the threadbare jacket he was wearing.

'They're expensive, the Boosey,' he said, sucking his teeth dramatically. 'Even second-hand.'

He paused to let it sink in, in case the boy was only messing about.

'Last one we had in here went for ... I don't know, eighty, ninety quid I should think. Something like that.'

The boy did not answer but looked steadily at Sapper.

'Not that we get many in,' Sapper went on, flustered by the boy's silence. 'That's probably only the second or third I've had here in, well ...'

The boy startled him by saying thank you and leaving without another word. Outside the rain had stopped, but the gutter was blocked and Sapper's pavement was flooded.

It was getting on for two o'clock the following Tuesday and Mr Sapper was closing early as usual when the boy drew up, propped his bike against the kerb and squeezed in through the gear stacked just inside the shop.

'You remembered where to stand your bike then,' Sapper said jovially. Finishing early always put him in a good mood. It felt like time stolen.

The boy looked blankly at him and then remembered. He smiled shyly.

'Can I have a look at the trumpet,' he said diffidently.

Sapper smiled at him and pushed through the clutter to get at the trumpet in the window.

'Why aren't you at school?' he said over his shoulder.

'Next to the old cash register,' the boy reminded him as Sapper searched for the instrument in the crowded window. 'I've got a verruca. I can't do games this afternoon, so I skipped it.'

Sapper located the trumpet in its plush-lined case and brought it over to the chest of drawers. He turned it to face the boy, who picked it up and examined it.

'You said it was a Boosey,' he said in an aggrieved tone.

'Did I?' Sapper said. 'When was that?'

'Last week, when I asked you about it,' the boy said,

balancing the trumpet in his playing hand. 'That's why it was expensive, you said.'

'Did I? Well, I must have thought it was,' Sapper said. 'What is it then?'

'It's one of those East German ones,' the boy said. 'They're OK, I suppose, but nothing like as good as a Boosey.'

He pumped the valves up and down.

'These are stiff too,' he said.

'It's been in the window a while,' Sapper said defensively. 'Collecting dust and fluff and I don't know what. It just needs a good clean, that's all.'

The boy nodded. He altered the tube extension and flicked the spit valve a couple of times.

'Well they aren't as good as the Boosey and Hawkes,' he said.

He lifted the lid of the little accessories box inside the case, found the mouthpiece and fitted it.

'And the mouthpiece is worn,' he said, fingering the metal where the plating was worn through.

'That won't make much difference,' Sapper said airily. 'It won't affect the sound, will it?'

The boy pushed the mouthpiece home and lifted the instrument to his lips.

'That's it, give us a tune,' Sapper said. 'Give it a good try.'

The boy fingered the valves, loosening them with imaginary scales and runs.

'How much is it?' he said.

Sapper turned away from the boy and pretended to arrange something on the top of the chest of drawers.

'Didn't I say?' he said innocently. 'I thought I said.'

'You did,' the boy said. 'But the price you gave was when you thought it was a B and H, and it isn't. So how much now?'

'Eighty, wasn't it?' Sapper said cautiously. He couldn't remember exactly what he'd said.

The boy shook his head.

'No, that was for it when you thought it was ...'

'A Boosey and Hawkes,' Sapper finished for him. 'That's right, and it isn't, so obviously we'll have to make a little adjustment, won't we?'

The boy relaxed visibly.

'But even so,' Sapper went on. 'Even if it isn't a B and H, trumpets aren't ten a penny you know. There's not many cheap second-hand ones about, and there's always a demand.'

Neither of them spoke for a moment and the only sound was the little click the valves made as the boy fingered them quickly.

'What about,' Sapper said thoughtfully. 'What about ... say ... fifty-five. How does that suit you? Fifty-five.'

The boy brought the trumpet to his lips and blew experimentally. Sapper, who knew nothing at all about playing any musical instrument, could tell straight away that the boy knew what he was doing. The note was long and steady and clear, scooping at the end into the kind of blues note that made Sapper think the boy was launching into Basin Street Blues. He followed the note with a series of rapid runs which rose into the upper octave, and then took the trumpet from his lips, flicked the spit valve, and put it down carefully in its box.

'I haven't got that much,' he said simply. 'I was thinking maybe ...'

'Suit yourself boy,' Sapper said, snapping the locks shut, cross at the thought the boy had been wasting his time. 'I can easily get that for it anytime.'

But he couldn't help feeling sorry for the lad.

He didn't see the boy again for a week, and then he saw him propped up against the window one evening about eight o'clock as he and Mrs Sapper were driving past the shop, which they sometimes did on fine evenings. It had occurred to Sapper a number of times that shifting the old trumpet might not be as easy as he had suggested to the boy, and that it might have been a better bet to have offered to keep it for him until he'd got the money together. If he'd offered it to the lad for a better price, he might even have sold it already. On the other hand, the boy was clearly still interested in it, and that made Sapper feel better. Even so, he made a mental resolution to offer it to the boy for a bit less next time he saw him.

And that was the following day. It was just before closing time when he came in with a paper boy's bag over his shoulder.

'Hello stranger,' Sapper said. 'Come for the trumpet have you?'

The boy shifted uncomfortably.

'I was wondering,' he began.

'Well?' Sapper encouraged him.

'I was wondering whether you'd put it by for me? You know, kind of reserve it until I've got the money to pay for it.'

'I see,' Sapper said. It was what he'd been going to propose, but he liked it better, coming from the lad. 'And when might that be?'

'Not long, I hope,' the boy said with a trace of animation. 'It depends.'

What it depended on was left unsaid, but Sapper guessed that it depended a lot on what other things the boy had to buy for himself out of his paper-round money. He looked as if he could do with a pair of shoes to start off with.

'You can have it for forty-five,' Sapper said. 'But that's my best price and don't keep me hanging around, OK?'

The boy smiled broadly for the first time and shook his head.

'I suppose you want to see it again, now you're here,' Sapper said indulgently. He quite liked the feeling of being indulgent.

The boy shook his head.

'No I won't, not now,' he said. 'I'll leave it until I can buy it properly.'

He turned to go.

'You will keep it for me, won't you?'

'Sure,' Sapper said with a smile. 'I'll put a little notice on it to say it's sold.'

The boy looked at him with the serious, steady look that Sapper had often noticed. Then he was gone.

'You said you'd save it for me!' the boy said indignantly, bursting into the shop late on Saturday afternoon.

Sapper got up from his armchair and the sports pages.

'And I have,' he said. 'What makes you think I haven't?'

'It's still in the window,' the boy said, aggrieved.

'That's right lad, but I know you've reserved it,' Sapper said, putting the paper down on the top of the chest of drawers. 'How's the saving going?'

The boy ignored his assurances and the question.

'Why don't you take it out, then there'll be no mistakes,' he demanded.

'Makes the window look more interesting,' Sapper said. He had also decided to leave it in the window so that if the boy failed, at least it was on display and might attract a different buyer. 'Besides,' he said cannily. 'Where else can I put it?'

'Out the back there,' The boy pointed. 'Or at least put a "reserved" sign on it.'

Sapper reached into the top drawer and took out a square of card and a thick pen.

'There you are boy, you do it,' he said.

The boy wrote reserved in block capitals on the card and then put it in the case with the trumpet.

'OK?' Sapper said.

The boy nodded and relaxed. Sapper went back to his paper and the boy turned over one or two of the paperback books.

'How long have you been playing the trumpet?' Sapper said over his spectacles.

The boy put down a huge plumber's wrench and turned

back to Sapper.

'Four years,' he said, 'I have lessons. At school.'

'Like it, do you?' Sapper said, smiling.

'I like it better than everything else,' the boy said with feeling. 'It's the only thing about school I do like.'

'And why are you so keen on this trumpet?' Sapper said. 'What's the matter with the one you've got?'

'I haven't got one of my own,' he said. 'I have to share one with another boy at school. We have to take it in turns to take it home and practise.'

'That's not very satisfactory, I can see that,' Sapper said sympathetically.

The boy smiled quickly.

'No, it isn't,' he said. 'Specially because he's a mucky little kid. He never cleans it properly after he's had his go on it.'

'Disgusting,' Sapper said, keeping a straight face. 'And what sort of things do you like playing?'

'The usual stuff,' the boy said. 'Practice bits, and bits for the exams. I play in the school band as well, but that's often just hymns for assembly.'

'So what do you like best,' Sapper said.

'Nat Gonella,' the boy said. 'I'd like to play like him.'

You could have knocked Sapper over with the proverbial. He hadn't heard Nat Gonella spoken of for years, and the last person he had expected to hear speak of him was a teenage boy. He remembered the sleeked-back, black hair, the crooning voice, the soaring trumpet solos.

'My dad's got some old records of Nat Gonella,' the boy explained. 'I've been listening to them since I was little. I think he's great.'

Sapper suddenly felt a rush of affection for this boy who had so carelessly, so unwittingly, brought back to life a part of him which he'd lost touch with, it seemed centuries ago.

'Well you'll have to practise, won't you?' he said with a broad grin.

During the summer holiday the boy was in and out of the

shop often. Sometimes they just sat and drank a cup of tea and gossipped, and sometimes the boy helped him carry in the stuff off the pavement and close up the shop. He rarely mentioned the trumpet and Sapper guessed that saving for it was proving more difficult than he had bargained for. They often talked about jazz though, and trumpet players especially. Sapper told him about all the great bands of the thirties and forties and the boy listened avidly. Sapper had heard them all - Woody Herman at the Coulston Hall, Geraldo, Ellington, even Glen Miller once, and Nat Gonella of course, whom he'd followed all over London from hall to hall for nearly six months. He could talk about them for hours, and often did, and the boy never tired of hearing about them.

Calling often, the boy quickly became acquainted with Sapper's routines in the shop, so that he soon felt confident in leaving the boy to give an eye while he nipped out to the bank, to the pub, or for a lunch date with Mrs Sapper. For his part, the boy slowly imposed some order on the shop so that finding things gradually became less a voyage of discovery and more a matter of logic. It wasn't a change that Mr Sapper necessarily liked, but he could see how much easier it made it to run the shop so he didn't complain.

The day Mr Sapper was seeing to his bees and one stung him he knew that the summer was about over. His arm swelled painfully and Mrs Sapper had to take him to hospital for treatment. He didn't go into the shop for more than a week and when he did return, what with one thing and another, he didn't give much thought to the boy. The weather was definitely turning, the children were back at school, and there were days when Sapper was glad to light the gas fire, sometimes not extinguishing it all day. He saw the boy briefly a couple of times in the weeks following his bee sting but he was always in a hurry. Once he stayed long enough to help get the stuff in off the pavement, but as the autumn unfolded, Mr Sapper felt the passing of the easy intimacy they had enjoyed during the summer.

One day, reaching for something in the window, he knocked against the trumpet case. He could tell it was empty and didn't need to flick up the catches to be sure. He shook his head slowly at the empty box and threw it into the corner. There was a customer who haggled with him over two china dogs, but his heart was not in it and he let them go at a ridiculous price. As soon as the customer had gone he closed the shop and walked home.

'Hello lad,' Sapper said. 'Haven't seen you for ages. How's tricks?'

The boy had dropped in after school unexpectedly one afternoon in November. Sapper had the gas fire on and its hiss made a comfortable backdrop to their conversation.

'Still saving are you?' Sapper looked steadily at the boy.

'You've found out, haven't you?' the boy said, unable to meet Sapper's eyes.

'Do you know what, my lad,' Sapper said quietly, all the disappointment he had felt welling up in him again. 'Do you know what I was going to do?'

The boy would not look at him.

'I was going to give you it. Give it to you for helping during the summer.'

Still the boy said nothing.

'Hell!' Sapper said angrily. 'What did I want with a manky old trumpet? I was going to give it to you, wasn't I?'

He heard the boy sniff and then start to cry.

'I'm sorry,' he said at last. 'I am, really. It just grew and grew on me. I wanted it so badly and I knew I couldn't save up enough to buy it, I'll bring it back tomorrow. Honestly.'

Sapper felt embarrassed at the boy's tears. He'd never seen someone so nearly a man cry before.

'You should have said,' he said, patting the boy's shoulder absently.

'Then you'd have sold it,' the boy said between sobs.

'If only you'd waited,' he said. 'I'd have given it to you.'

'I didn't know,' the boy cried.

The shop was silent except for the hiss of the gas.

'Consider it wages,' Sapper said after a moment, in his briskest voice. 'Wages for the summer.'

He paused to let the boy recover.

'Come on now,' he said. 'Get the things in off the kerb will you?'

The boy wiped his eyes on his sleeve and went to the door. Sapper turned abruptly and went into the back of the shop.

The Great Leapfrog Contest

by William Saroyan

Rosie Mahoney was a tough little Irish kid whose folks, through some miscalculation in directions, or out of an innate spirit of anarchy, had moved into the Russian-Italian-and-Greek neighbourhood of my home town, across the Southern Pacific tracks, around G Street.

She wore a turtle-neck sweater, usually red. Her father was a bricklayer named Cull and a heavy drinker. Her mother's name was Mary. Mary Mahoney used to go to the Greek Orthodox Catholic Church on Kearny Boulevard every Sunday, because there was no Irish Church to go to anywhere in the neighbourhood. The family seemed to be a happy one.

Rosie's three brothers had all grown up and gone to sea. Her two sisters had married. Rosie was the last of the clan. She had entered the world when her father had been close to sixty and her mother in her early fifties. For all that, she was hardly the studious or scholarly type.

Rosie had little use for girls, and as far as possible avoided them. She had less use for boys, but found it undesirable to avoid them. That is to say, she made it a point to take part in everything the boys did. She was always on hand, and always the first to take up any daring or crazy idea. Everybody felt awkward about her continuous presence, but it was no use trying to chase her away, because that meant a fight in which she asked no quarter, and gave none.

If she didn't whip every boy she fought, every fight was at least an honest draw, with a slight edge in Rosie's favour. She didn't fight girl-style, or cry if hurt. She fought the regular style and took advantage of every opening. It was very humiliating to be hurt by Rosie, so after a while any boy who thought of trying to chase her away, decided not to.

It was no use. She just wouldn't go. She didn't seem to like any of the boys especially, but she liked being in on any mischief they might have in mind, and she wanted to play on any teams they organized. She was an excellent baseball player, being as good as anybody else in the neighbourhood at any position, and for her age an expert pitcher. She had a wicked wing, too, and could throw a ball in from left field so that when it hit the catcher's mitt it made a nice sound.

She was extraordinarily swift on her feet and played a beautiful game of tin-can hockey.

At pee-wee, she seemed to have the most disgusting luck in the world.

At the game we invented and used to call Horse she was as good at horse as at rider, and she insisted on following the rules of the game. She insisted on being horse when it was her turn to be horse. This always embarrassed her partner, whoever he happened to be, because it didn't seem right for a boy to be getting up on the back of a girl.

She was an excellent football player too.

As a matter of fact, she was just naturally the equal of any boy in the neighbourhood, and much the superior of many of them. Especially after she had lived in the neighbourhood three years. It took her that long to make everybody understand that she had come to stay and that she was going to stay.

She did, too; even after the arrival of a boy named Rex Folger, who was from somewhere in the south of Texas. This boy Rex was a natural-born leader. Two months after his arrival in the neighbourhood, it was understood by everyone that if Rex wasn't the leader of the gang, he was very nearly the leader. He had fought and licked every boy in the neighbourhood who at one time or another had fancied himself leader. And he had done so without any noticeable ill-feeling, pride, or ambition.

As a matter of fact, no-one could possibly have been more good-natured than Rex. Everybody resented him, just the same.

One winter, the whole neighbourhood took to playing a game that had become popular on the other side of the track, in another slum neighbourhood of the town: Leapfrog.

The idea was for as many boys as cared to participate, to bend down and be leaped over by every other boy in the game, and then himself to get up and begin leaping over all the other boys, and then bend down again until all the boys had leaped over him again, and keep this up until all the other players had become exhausted. This didn't happen, sometimes, until the last two players had travelled a distance of three or four miles, while the other players walked along, watching and making bets.

Rosie, of course, was always in on the game. She was always one of the last to drop out, too. And she was the only person in the neighbourhood Rex Folger hadn't fought and beaten.

He felt that that was much too humiliating even to think about. But inasmuch as she seemed to be a member of the gang, he felt that in some way or another he ought to prove his superiority.

One summer day during vacation, an argument between Rex and Rosie developed and Rosie pulled off her turtle-neck sweater and challenged him to a fight. Rex took a cigarette from his pocket, lighted it, inhaled, and told Rosie he wasn't in the habit of hitting women - where he came from that amounted to boxing your mother. On the other hand, he said, if Rosie cared to compete with him in any other sport, he would be glad to oblige her. Rex was a very calm and courteous conversationalist. He had poise. It was unconscious, of course, but he had it just the same. He was just naturally a man who couldn't be hurried, flustered, or excited.

So Rex and Rosie fought it out in this game Leapfrog. They got to leaping over one another, quickly, too until the first thing we knew the whole gang of us was out on the State Highway going south towards Fowler. It was a very hot day. Rosie and Rex were in great shape, and it looked like one was no tougher than the other and more stubborn. They talked a good deal, especially Rosie, who insisted that she would have to fall down unconscious before she'd give up to a guy like Rex.

He said he was sorry his opponent was a girl. It grieved him deeply to have to make a girl exert herself to the point of death, but it was just too bad. He had to, so he had to. They leaped and squatted, leaped and squatted, and we got out to Sam Day's vineyard. That was half-way to Fowler. It didn't seem like either Rosie or Rex was ever going to get tired. They hadn't even begun to show signs of growing tired, although each of them was sweating a great deal.

Naturally, we were sure Rex would win the contest. But that was because we hadn't taken into account the fact that he was a simple person, whereas Rosie was crafty and shrewd. Rosie knew how to figure angles. She had discovered him. After a while, about three miles out of Fowler, we noticed that she was coming down on Rex's neck, instead of on his back. Naturally, this was hurting him and making the blood rush to his head. Rosie herself squatted in such a way that it was impossible, almost, for Rex to get anywhere near her neck with his hands.

Before long, we noticed that Rex was weakening. His head was getting closer and closer to the ground. About half a mile out of Fowler, we heard Rex's head bumping the ground every time Rosie leaped over him. They were good loud bumps that we knew were painful, but Rex wasn't complaining. He was too proud to complain.

Rosie, on the other hand, knew she had her man, and she was giving him all she had. She was bumping his head on the ground as solidly as she could, because she knew she didn't have much more fight in her, and if she didn't lay him out cold, in the hot sun, in the next ten minutes or so, she would fall down exhausted herself, and lose the contest.

Suddenly Rosie bumped Rex's head a real powerful one. He got up very dazed and very angry. It was the first time we had ever seen him fuming. By God, the girl was taking advantage of him, if he wasn't mistaken, and he didn't like it. Rosie was squatted in front of him. He came up groggy and paused a moment. Then he gave Rosie a very effective kick that sent her sprawling. Rosie jumped up and smacked Rex in the mouth. The gang jumped in and tried to establish order.

It was agreed that the Leapfrog contest must not change into a fight. Not any more. Not with Fowler only five or ten minutes away. The gang ruled further that Rex had had no right to kick Rosie and that in smacking him in the mouth Rosie had squared the matter, and the contest was to continue.

Rosie was very tired and sore; and so was Rex. They began leaping and squatting again; and again we saw Rosie coming down on Rex's neck so that his head was bumping the ground.

It looked pretty bad for the boy from Texas. We couldn't understand how he could take so much punishment. We all felt that Rex was getting what he had coming to him, but at the same time everybody seemed to feel badly about Rosie, a girl, doing the job instead of one of us. Of course, that was where we were wrong. Nobody but Rosie could have figured out that smart way of humiliating a very powerful and superior boy. It was probably the woman in her, which, less than five years later, came out to such an extent that she became one of the most beautiful girls in town, gave up tomboy activities, and married one of the wealthiest young men in Kings County, a college man named, if memory serves, Wallace Hadington Finlay VI.

Less than a hundred yards from the heart of Fowler, Rosie, with great and admirable artistry, finished the job.

That was where the dirt of the highway siding ended and the paved main street of Fowler began. This street was paved with cement, not asphalt. Asphalt, in that heat, would have been too soft to serve, but cement had exactly the right degree of brittleness. I think Rex, when he squatted over the hard cement, knew the game was up. But he was brave to the end. He squatted over the hard cement and waited for the worst. Behind him, Rosie Mahoney prepared to make the supreme effort. In this next leap, she intended to give her all, which she did.

She came down on Rex Folger's neck like a ton of bricks. His head banged against the hard cement, his body straightened out, and his arms and legs twitched.

He was out like a light.

Six paces in front of him. Rosie Mahoney squatted and waited. Jim Telesco counted twenty, which was the time allowed for each leap. Rex didn't get up during the count.

The contest was over. The winner of the contest was Rosie Mahoney.

Rex didn't get up by himself at all. He just stayed where he was until a half-dozen of us lifted him and carried him to a horse trough, where we splashed water on his face.

Rex was a confused young man all the way back. He was also a deeply humiliated one. He couldn't understand anything about anything. He just looked dazed and speechless. Every now and then we imagined he wanted to talk, and I guess he did, but after we'd all gotten ready to hear what he had to say, he couldn't speak. He made a gesture so tragic that tears came to the eyes of eleven members of the gang.

Rosie Mahoney, on the other hand, talked all the way home. She said everything.

I think it made a better man of Rex. More human. After that he was a gentler sort of soul. It may have been because he couldn't see very well for some time. At any rate, for weeks he seemed to be going around in a dream. His gaze would freeze on some insignificant object far away in the landscape, and half the time it seemed as if he didn't know where he was going, or why. He took little part in the activities of the gang, and the following winter he stayed away altogether. He came to school one day wearing glasses. He looked broken and pathetic.

That winter Rosie Mahoney stopped hanging around with the gang, too. She had a flair for making an exit at the right time.

Owls are Night Birds

by Berlie Doherty

Elaine was always a little in front of Steven as they scrambled up the slope. It was so steep that they had to heave themselves up by clinging on to the coarse sprouting grass. When Elaine hauled herself up at last on to the top path she stood watching Steven, not helping him, as loose stones scuttled under his feet.

'Hot!' she gasped. 'Too hot!'

The path was dusty and rutted. It would lead them through the donkey field, past the new housing estate and the infant school, and on up the hill to their home.

'Come on, Steven.' Elaine set off again as soon as her brother had pulled himself over the tip of the slope. For a moment he lay on the grass at the side of the path, listening to the thud of her feet. Far away he could hear the drone of the city, like a hushed roar. The sound never stopped, day and night. It was the sound of foundries, hammering like a heart. It was the sound of cars and lorries and buses, always on the move, like blood pumping through veins. It was the sound of half a million people breathing.

He felt as if he was drowning in the stale air of the city's breath. 'I'm a lizard,' he thought. 'I'll dry up here in the sun; then she'll be sorry.' He stood up and ran along after her, stooping to search through the dense foliage for bilberries. He found some that the birds had left, and crouched down so he could cram them into his mouth. 'They're saving my life,' he thought. 'She'll die.'

'I'm sick of you,' his sister shouted, impatient. 'Come on. I'll buy you some lemonade at Mr Dyson's, if you hurry.'

'Race you to the donkey field!' he yelled, and she took up his challenge and broke into a loose run as the path flattened and swung into the shelter of overhanging trees. He stumbled after her, his shoes slapping the hard earth, watching the swing of her yellow hair. 'Can't make it. I'm a dead man.' He nursed a stitch that bent him sideways. He watched Elaine as she clambered up the leaning stone wall that surrounded the donkey field. She held herself there, motionless, with her hand lifted to shield her eyes. He limped up to her, drawing in his breath and groaning so that she wouldn't laugh at him for losing the race, but she swung her arm behind her in a warning gesture, and he pulled himself up beside her and sat with his legs straddling the hump of the wall; silent.

He saw immediately what she was looking at. A large white bird moved across the field towards them; a bird with a broad heavy head and wide blunt wings. It swung upwards, its great wings driving it like a swimmer through still water, and it drifted, bullet-headed, a huge silent moth, lifting itself soundlessly, while the air hung quiet around it. In the middle of the field the donkeys pressed and nudged each other, flicking their ears idly, unconscious of the dark shadow gliding over them.

'What is it?'

'It's an owl,' said Elaine softly. She couldn't take her eyes off it.

Steven slid off the wall and lay with the long grass criss-crossed over him. 'But owls are night birds.' He followed the slow flight of the bird quartering the field. With a last wide sweep that swung it high above their heads it left the field and floated across the wide valley, and was lost among the dark trees that shadowed the river on the far side; miles away.

Elaine slid down beside him and they trudged across the field. Steven pointed out some deep trenches that had been cut across the far end. They stretched out in a line from the end of the housing estate to the village lane, and they seemed to be huge squares dug into the soil. They walked slowly round them.

'What d'you think these are?' Steven asked. 'Why should someone dig up the donkey field?'

'I dunno,' said Elaine. 'Donkeys had better watch it, or they'll drop in.'

They both giggled.

'Come on,' said Steven. 'Let's ask Mr Dyson about that bird.'

He raced away from her, and she followed him slowly, her mind on the great white bird with sunlight like cream across its back.

Mr Dyson's corner shop was at the end of the lane that led up to their house. From there he'd sold sweets and drinks to generations of children on their way to and from school. You could hardly call it a shop now. At one time it had been crammed with ropes and buckets and bacon and socks and all the oddments that people in a village might want to buy in a hurry. But then, a few years ago, old Mr Dyson had had a stroke, and the village people had started going down to the supermarket that had opened up on the main road down to the city. Mr Dyson's stroke had left him partially paralysed. He never went out any more. His wife had kept the shop going so that at least he'd see the people who came in to buy, and they were mostly children, who knew that they could spend all the time in the world making their choices. She baked daily, and the warm sweet smell of new-baked bread and cakes snapped at you as you came up the hill, drawing you in. The shop part was really their front room, and at the jingle of the bell, old Mr Dyson would struggle out of the back room and greet the visitor with a shout of pleasure.

'I'll give you some money,' Elaine said. 'I'll wait out here.' Steven pulled her in. She was frightened of Mr Dyson now. His body was curiously twisted, so that one arm hung useless and one leg dragged to the side, and he walked with a laborious hopping rock-shuffle. His speech slurred one consonant into the other, making it impossible for anyone to understand him without watching his eyes, and Elaine was frightened of doing this. Usually she pushed her money across the counter to him and took her sweets and ran, letting the door jangle shut behind her and breathing in the outside air. But Steven loved him. He would climb on to the high stool that was put out for people who couldn't choose their sweets in a hurry and he and Mr Dyson would struggle to talk to each other. Sometimes, if they got stuck, Mrs

Dyson would come out from the back and translate for them. She was sad and old and little, and hardly ever smiled.

Today Mr Dyson was dispirited. He leaned across the counter with his good arm, flapping his hand at the wasps that buzzed above the sticky cakes.

'Hey! Mr Dyson!' Steven shouted as he ran in.

The old man looked up, pleased. 'Hey! Hey!' he shouted back, and nodded to the cane stool. 'What have you two been up to today?' he seemed to say. You could just tell by the vowels.

'Mr Dyson! Wait till I tell you what we've seen!'

Elaine hung back. After the brilliance of the summer sunshine the shop was dark and gloomy. It was as if all that daylight no longer existed. She hated the dim stuffiness of the place. She watched the strip of yellow sticky paper that hung from the light bulb above the counter. It was stuck with the dead and dying bodies of wasps and flies and bluebottles, and it swivelled round slowly with the draught of air they'd brought in with them from outside. She longed to dive back out into the sunlight again.

'It was a bird, Mr Dyson, a great white one, like a ghost.'

'Like an owl,' said Elaine, cross.

'But it couldn't have been an owl, could it? They're night birds.'

Elaine wanted to tell him about the strange coldness it had put on them. Maybe that was what Steven had meant.

Mr Dyson frowned and nodded and called his wife in to help him out, and she came in with a jug of home-made lemonade that was all frothy and cloudy and swimming with pips, and poured some out for the two children.

'Come on Elaine,' she said, and Elaine edged forward and sat awkwardly on the other chair. The woman watched her husband as he talked, and spoke to him in the same sort of brief unfinished words. He seemed very tired, and kept shifting his position. The children drank, watching them.

'He reckons it's a barn owl,' Mrs Dyson said at last. 'An albino barn owl. A bit of a freak. That's why it's so white.

And if its hearing and eyesight are weak, then it can't hunt by night, so it has to come out by day when seeing's easier. Fancy, he says, by all them new houses.'

Mr Dyson muttered something again and she translated it, but Steven beat her to it with a laugh of triumph.

'He says we're a pair of lucky jiggers to see it, an' all.'

Mr Dyson shook his head and swung his heavy body round, as if he were tired of this conversation, and heaved himself into the back room. His wife took the glasses from the children and put them on her tray.

'When he was a young man,' she told them quietly, 'he liked nothing better than to be up walking in the hills. You could walk for miles in them days, either direction, and still be in the country. And birds was his hobby, watching birds all hours, when he was young, and well.'

'We saw something else as well,' Steven said. 'Big holes. In the field.'

Mrs Dyson shook her head at him and looked quickly towards the back room, as if making sure that her husband hadn't heard. Then she took the tray into the back without saying goodbye, and Steven and Elaine left their money on the counter and went outside, squeezing past the door so they didn't make the shop bell jangle.

A few days later Elaine and Steven went back to the donkey field, and there was the barn owl again.

'Barney!' Steven whispered, watching it.

They both felt the same thrill of excitement and strange surge of uneasiness as the air became silent and the bird moved strongly and soundlessly round them, and at last drifted away to its home.

'Tell him! I'm going to tell him!' Steven shouted. His heart was thudding with excitement as he raced out of the field to Mr Dyson's shop. Elaine trailed after him, and stopped to look at the holes in the earth. They were deeper now. They were proper trenches, roped off in big squares. A huge yellow fork-lift truck was parked by the gate, and beyond it, a workmen's portacabin. She walked down past the end hole square. After that was the new road, and beyond that, the housing estate. She could see nothing but houses from there, spreading down the long hill in a pattern of pink and grey roofs, down, down, to the far throbbing valley that was the heart of the city.

'Hey!' Mr Dyson laughed as Steven burst into the shop.

'Hey!' said Steven. 'We've seen it again!'

Mr Dyson chuckled as he listened to Steven, indicating that he wanted him to crawl under the counter flap and to come through with him to the back of the cottage. Mrs Dyson was baking. The room was neat and small, and as dark as the shop. Mr Dyson knelt down on one knee with his bad leg stretched behind him and searched through a pile of oddments under the table. At last he fished out what he was looking for. It was a large book.

'Bird Journal,' Steven read. 'Is this from when you were young and well, Mr Dyson?'

Mrs Dyson swung round to chastise him, but the old man chuckled and fingered through the carefully handwritten pages with their listings and sketches of birds he'd observed. He folded the book back on its first clean page.

'Pen, love,' he sounded to his wife, and she, floury and smiling now, found him one.

'Barn owl', he wrote.

'Barney,' Steven told him, and Mr Dyson wrote it in brackets next to the heading. 'Sighted, 3 p.m. Friday, August 3rd and Tuesday, August 7th. The donkey field.'

Mrs Dyson found some pencils and Steven sketched the owl in flight, and when he left Mr Dyson was sitting at the kitchen table, his tongue pressed out between his teeth like a child's, shading in Steven's sketch with coloured pencils.

Elaine was waiting for Steven outside the shop. 'They're building,' she told him.

'Building?' he repeated, puzzled.

'In the donkey field. They're building something there.'

'They can't,' he said flatly. 'It's the last bit of country left before the city. They can't build there.'

'Anyway,' he thought. 'It belongs to Barney now, that field.'

From then on the donkey field was Steven's favourite haunt. Elaine went with him a couple of times but by the time she'd seen Barney twice more she was bored. At least, that's what she told Steven. She loved to watch the owl's slow flight, but she hated the drone of the trucks and building lorries down at the bottom of the field, and the loud shouts of the workmen. She hated what she was seeing, as the earth holes were filled in with cement and tons of red bricks were tipped out nearby.

And she dreaded the visits to Mr Dyson's afterwards. The dimness and the stuffiness of the shop closed round her like winter nights, chasing away the summer. She felt strangely as if the donkey field and Barney were things they'd made up for the old man's benefit. For the first time ever, Steven and Elaine started to drift apart. They didn't even realise it was happening.

'Coming to the donkey field?' Steven asked her one day. She shrugged and followed him slowly out of the house, and then just didn't bother to go down the road after him, and he didn't bother to go back for her. She watched him running off down the hill, and couldn't explain the sadness she felt inside herself. She rang up a school friend and arranged to meet her in town, and they spent that day and most of the rest of the holiday touring the boutiques and trying on new clothes. She wanted to look like the city girls, who always looked fresh and bright. She was sick of the country clothes she wore at home, all faded cottons and old jeans. They made her look too young.

'Guess what my brother's doing now?' she said to her friend, Anna, one day. 'He's lying in a donkey field.'

'What for?' Anna asked, astonished.

'Watching a silly old owl!'

The two girls exploded into giggles, and turned themselves round in front of the shop mirror, admiring themselves in the dresses they couldn't afford to buy.

Mr Dyson loved Steven's visits. He wrote up his journal every day. Once Steven found an owl pellet near the trees and carried it, warm in his hand to the old man; a trophy, to the dark room where Mr Dyson had imprisoned himself. They rolled it open and sketched the tiny mouse bones they found in it. Mr Dyson had long forgotten the misery and resentment he'd felt when he first heard about Barney. The pellet was his find now, just as much as it was Steven's.

Sometimes Mrs Dyson would stand at the doorway of the shop watching out for Steven. 'Come on, love! He's waiting!' she'd sing out, and she'd leave the shop door propped open to let in the daylight. She brought flowers into the house and bustled round them while they talked, or sat, listening peacefully to their strange and awkward conversations. For the first time in years she forgot to be worried about her husband. She coaxed him into their little back garden where he could sit out and watch the cloud patterns on the far hills, and read the bird books Steven brought him from the library. And whenever Steven came there was always a glass of golden ginger beer or pale lemonade or apple juice for him, and new scones spread with home-made jam with strawberries whole and plump in it.

Sometimes they heard trucks trundling past on their way to the field. They seemed to make the whole cottage shake. Mr Dyson would look at his wife, worried and questioning, and she would look at Steven, willing him to keep his mouth shut. Steven always stopped to look at the buildings as he came past. The squares of bricks were as high as his waist now, and there was a gap in the front and the back of every one of them, just wide enough for someone to go in and out.

And then Barney left the field. Day after day Steven ran down there and lay in the long grass scanning the sky. He would race down on his way to the big shops on the estate, or first thing in the morning, or early evening, and the donkeys would always trot over and nuzzle him. But he hadn't come for the donkeys, or for the looping swallows. He was convinced that the albino owl had died. One day the donkeys were gone from the field too, and another row of trenches had been dug. He ran down to the first lot of buildings. The lines of bricks were higher. Rectangular spaces were left on all the sides. The holes that were big enough to walk in and out of were covered over at the top, and he knew for the first time what he had known in his heart for weeks. 'Doors!' he said out loud. 'Houses! They've joined us up with the city.'

He picked up a handful of rubble and started chucking it through the doorways and window holes, enjoying the thud of it as it spattered against the inside walls.

'Oi!' One of the builders yelled at him. 'What you up to? Eh?'

'You've killed Barney!' Steven shouted. 'This is his hunting field. You've killed him!'

The man shouted at him to clear off, and Steven ran home, straight past Mr Dyson's shop, not even looking. For the next few days he kept going down to the field, just in case, and he came slowly past the shop. Sometimes he just tapped on the window and shook his head.

He spent all Saturday in the field when the workmen were not working. He wandered miserably round the buildings, wondering if he could get the cement mixer to work, thinking about filling in all the door and window holes, and he knew that it was useless. The city had come, and there was no stopping it. He heard a great roar surge up from somewhere far below, and he ran to the edge of the field, listening. It was the sound of a football match. It was a goal. He heard the excited chanting of the Crown and found his own voice in it, 'Ci-ty! Ci-ty! Ci-ty!' he murmured, and then louder and louder, yelling it out, a thrill of excitement inside him. 'Ci-ty!'

And that was the last day of the summer holidays. He and Elaine started back at school the next week. They never sat together on the bus any more. She had her own friends now.

Mr Dyson sat all day at his table, waiting for the boy to come. He listened inside himself for Steven's animated chatter that had brought so much of the summer sunshine into his dark home. His house had grown gloomy and quiet again. He was lost for things to do, and Mrs Dyson became anxious and unsmiling again, watching him. He kept his journal open and ready on the table, and at the end of the day he would write with his good hand, 'No Barney today.'

'No Steven today,' Mrs Dyson would say, looking over his shoulder. That was what he meant.

When the letter came from the council telling them that the cottages in their lane were to be demolished to make way for the new development she hid it in fear from him. She spent hours in her garden, pulling up weeds uselessly. 'It's coming, it's coming,' she said to herself. 'There's no stopping cities.' They'd have a modern house with proper facilities. They'd be surrounded. It would make a change. It would break the old man's heart.

The last day in September was brilliantly sunny. Steven and Elaine had nothing to do, and decided to go down to the river together. Steven was shy about asking Elaine to come with him now. They picnicked there and she lay back, catching a last suntan, while Steven skimmed pebbles on the water and watched the wagtails and dippers bobbing on the stony banks. They'd come the long way because that would bring them back on their favourite walk past the farm with the goats and eventually, up the long hill to the donkey field. They didn't mention Barney to each other. He belonged to a part of the summer that was past.

'Race you to the donkey field!' he challenged as they panted up the slope.

'Not a donkey field now!' she reminded him. 'Housing estate.'

They scrambled up the last steep slope and Elaine swung along the path, with Steven close behind her, and as they clambered up the stone wall there it was again; the white owl, in the full brilliance of the late afternoon: Barney. Low over the grass, and below them, with its broad strong head and its pale soft back, quartering the field of half-grown houses with slow lifts of its wings. There was no other movement in the field. Not a sound.

Elaine and Steven stood, breathless, on the wall, following Barney's route across the field, and suddenly Steven's eyes were stopped by an unfamiliar bundle in the grass, a twist of drab colour, humped at an angle. He turned sharply to Elaine and she smiled and nodded and laid her hand on his arm. Mr Dyson, lying in the long grass at the side of the field, raised his arm slowly as if in a salute, and rested his hand as a shield above his eyes, watching the movements of the daylight owl.

Steven thought of the old man dragging himself to the front of his shop; his slow unsteady shuffle. It must have taken him hours to get himself down the lane, past the little school, through all the rubble of the building site and across the rough grass to where he lay now, folded in a corner of the field. He forgot to watch Barney, and when he looked again the bird was making its last circle of the field. It rose higher and higher, right into the line of the sun, nearly blinding him, and then it drifted out across the valley to its dark shelter. Steven knew that he would never see it again.

The voice of the city surged up like a throaty roar and died away again. Steven plunged across the grass to the old man.

'What d'you think of Barney. Mr Dyson? I told you, didn't I?'

Mr Dyson lay with his hand still resting across his eyes, like a small child suddenly fallen asleep. The boy stood back a little, and his sister joined him. Together they looked down at the old man, with the grass criss-crossed against his face, and the small bees droning round him, and the sun warm on him.

Elaine put her arm round Steven's shoulder.

'We'd better go,' she told him. 'We'd better tell her.'

'But, he isn't asleep, is he?' said Steven doubtfully, staring down at the old man, at the humped twist of his body and the strange expression of peace on his face.

'No. He isn't asleep. He's all right.'

And the brother and sister walked slowly from their summer field in silence together.

Follow-on

A Present from the Hartz Mountains

by Gene Kemp

About the story

Some of us drift into sleep at night dreaming of exciting journeys through space where we meet unusual creatures and discover strange planets, or of daring adventures on the Spanish Main where we fight to the death with ferocious pirates and find the buried treasure. When David trips over the tree root and bumps his head he enters a world of make believe - or does he? Perhaps the witch with the green hooky nose and red shiny eyes really exists!

Talk it over

1 What makes this story such an interesting, exciting and funny one?

2 How do David and Jill get on together? Is it a typical brother-sister relationship? If you have a brother or a sister what sort of things do you argue about?

3 In this story Jill and Jonathan walk into the television screen and enter the world of the gingerbread witch. If you could do the same, what television programmes would you like to join?

4 Below is a list of words. Which ones do you think best describe the characters in this story:

friendly	outgoing	kind
intelligent	shy	quick-tempered
amusing	sarcastic	clumsy
silly	even-tempered	kind
witty	lively	tolerant
unkind	courageous	bossy

5 Imagine that you have been given the task of turning this short story into a television play. Discuss what would make good television and where there would be problems. What changes would you make? What do the various characters look like?

Write it down

1 `The trouble is, nobody believes me.' Use this opening sentence for a story or short play of your own.

2 Write a poem, play or short story about a school outing.

3 From the little we know about her, Aunt Kate seems to be rather eccentric and amusing. Write a description of her, imagining what she looks like, the kind of things she enjoys doing and something about her personality.

4 Write the letter David might have sent to Aunt Kate thanking her for the presents and relating the incredible adventure.

5 The following week David and Jill receive another present from Aunt Kate, this time from the Swiss Alps. It is an ugly little wooden troll. Write another exciting and fantastic story.

Act it out

1 It is two-fifteen when the children arrive at the monkey house. Their angry teacher demands to know why they are late. Act out the scene. Other characters might include the keeper of the monkey house, visitors to the zoo, the other children on the school outing.

2 In groups, record *A Present from the Hartz Mountains* in the form of a radio story. You might make your recording more interesting by including opening and closing music and sound effects. You might like to re-write the story as a radio play.

Further reading

Children love Gene Kemp's books: they are lively, extremely funny and very entertaining and she has written lots. Her novels and short stories include the *Tamworth Pig* series for younger children, *The Turbulent Term of Tyke Tyler* and *Gowie Corby Plays Chicken*; *Ducks and Dragons*, a poetry anthology; and *Dog Days and Cat Naps*, a collection of short stories.

The Ceremony

by Martyn Copus

About the story

All of us look forward to pleasant occasions like birthdays, Christmas and holidays by the sea. Sometimes, however, future events such as going into hospital for an operation, or an appointment with the Headteacher on Monday morning, fill us with dread. In this amusing story Terry Williams desperately wants to be one of the gang, but thoughts of the initiation ceremony which he will have to undergo make him more and more worried and afraid. He little realises what is in store for him.

Talk it over

1 What signs are there at the beginning which tell the reader that this is going to be an amusing story?

2 What do you learn about Terry from this story? Would you like to have him for a friend or a brother? Give reasons for your answer.

3 Terry is made to do something extremely unpleasant by members of the gang. Sometimes children can be hurtful and play cruel jokes on one another. Have you ever been the victim of an unpleasant trick?

4 Discuss other appropriate titles for this short story.

5 What is your reaction to the way this story ends? Did you think it would end in this way?

Write it down

1 Rewrite the story, imagining that Arthur is telling it.

2 As the time of the ceremony approaches, Terry becomes more and more fearful and imagines all sorts of horrors. Have you ever been anxious and afraid about something which is about to happen? Can you remember your thoughts and feelings at the time? After the event, was it as bad as you imagined? Write a short account called `The time I was most afraid.'

3 'It was just like any other day really. But all the time I felt something ought to happen. You know, something very unusual.' Use this as the opening paragraph to an amusing and exciting story of your own called: 'A day to remember!'

4 Most gangs have rules. Write the list of rules for the gang Terry joins. Think of an unusual and colourful name for the gang. What is the secret sign only members know?

5 Write a further episode in the adventures of Terry, Arthur and the gang.

Act it out

1 Act out the scene when Terry, feeling and looking ill, arrives home after the ceremony. Your play might begin where Terry's mother asks where he has been. Other characters in your play could include Terry's grandma or grandad, a neighbour, a brother or sister.

2 At the next meeting of the gang in the old house on the edge of the railway, the members hear footsteps, then they see a shadow at the window. The door creaks open and .... Act out the scene.

3 Miss Craddock's class is interrupted the following morning by the Headteacher and a policeman. They wish to speak to any pupil who was down by the railway line the previous afternoon. What happens?

Further reading

The Ceremony is the first in a lively and very funny collection of short stories about Terry Williams, who never seems to be out of trouble. The stories are full of colourful characters, exciting escapades and hilarious adventures and are well worth reading.

A Mother in Mannville

by Marjorie Kinnan Rawlings

About the story

We all tell tall stories at some time in our lives. It might be to amuse others or to conceal something we have done. Sometimes it could be to cover our embarrassment, disappointment or fear. In this sad and very moving short story, an orphan meets a famous writer and he weaves a story of his own.

Talk it over

1 What do you learn about Jerry from this story? Why do you think he invented the story about his mother?

2 What picture do you have of the orphanage from the details given in the story?

3 What is your impression of the story teller? What do you think are her feelings when she learns Jerry has no mother?

4 Can you guess what is going through Jerry's mind when he learns Miss Rawlings is leaving?

5 At the end Miss Clark says: `He has no mother. He has no skates.' Discuss what she might have gone on to say.

Write it down

1 Write about an occasion when you, or someone you know, have invented a story.

2 The writer, in a few short lines, captures the moods of the various seasons high in the Carolina mountains. Write a short description of the place where you live at a particular time of year. Think of the sounds, colours and smells. You may like to write your description as a short poem like Dean, who lives in a mining village in South Yorkshire.

Winter

The dark slagheaps are now slopes of white,
No sludge or mud or dust or coke.

The ground is crunchy clean and bright
And the air sharp with icy smoke.
The rows of terraced houses look the same
Blanketed in snow, a long white line,
And muffled figures on their way to work
Forget about the coal dust and the grime.
The sky is empty, pearl grey, clean
And the pale gold moon can hardly gleam.

3 Re-write the story, imagining that Jerry is telling it.

4 Suppose that Miss Rawlings had written to Jerry when she had arrived in Mexico. Write the letters they might have exchanged.

5 Write about the next few weeks in Jerry's life.

Act it out

1 Imagine that you are Jerry. You arrive back at the orphanage later that day. Act out the scene in which Miss Clark informs you about Miss Rawlings' visit and then tells you off for telling lies. Other pupils in your class could play the parts of the children in the orphanage.

2 Imagine that you are Miss Rawlings. You visit the orphanage a year later. What happens?

3 Imagine that Jerry does not return that night. Make up a play about his disappearance. Characters in your play could include Miss Clark, Miss Rawlings, Jerry's friends, the police, members of the search party, a newspaper reporter.

Further reading

Marjorie Kinnan Rawlings is a famous American writer whose best known story *The Yearling* is one of the most popular children's novels. It is a beautifully written and exciting story about Jody Baxter, a farmer's young son, and about his courage and determination.

Yellow Bird

by John Latham

About the story

We are all tempted at some time to do something we know we shouldn't and which we later regret. We then have to face the consequences of our actions. The boy in this story is told by his mother not to let the old lady's canary out of its cage, but he just has to do it. What happens then is unexpected and tragic.

Talk it over

1 Did you find this story funny, sad, disturbing, irritating, puzzling?

2 Can you remember a time when you did something on the spur of the moment which you later regretted?

3 What sort of person is the boy who is telling the story? Think about his looks, personality, likes and dislikes, his family, and the way he sees the world.

4 At what point in the story did you first realise that it is set just after the Second World War? What other clues help you to decide when the events took place?

5 Mrs Mallion speaks a Lancashire dialect. She uses certain words like `yossack' and `lommer' you might not recognise and she speaks with an accent you may find difficult to understand in places.

Find out the difference between accent and dialect.

Read the following four comments about the way people speak and share your views on this topic. You might like to discuss the words, phrases and pronunciations that your own dialect contains.

'The way people speak is important. If you speak with a posh accent, sort of la-di-da, people take a lot of notice of you. They think that you're clever and have a good job and a lot of money. If you speak in a common voice people think you're stupid and don't have a very good job and are poor.'

Catherine Heptonstall

'I like the different ways people speak. It makes life more interesting. When you travel around the country you hear lots of different accents. Scottish is my favourite. I don't like the Birmingham accent or the Northern Irish. I think it is a good thing that we all speak in different ways. It would be boring if we all spoke the same.'

Lesley Connerton

'When I moved down South I hated it at first. Every time I spoke people laughed at me or mimicked the way I spoke. I used to say "gi'oer" for "give over" or "stop it", and "tha" instead of "you", and I pronounced words like "butter" and "path" and "bath" in a different way from everyone else. They used to say: "batter" and "paath". I think it would be a lot better if everyone spoke the same. Then you wouldn't have people making fun of the way that others speak.'

John Farmer

Write it down

1 Write a short story based on one of the following lines taken from *Yellow Bird*:

No-one would ever know
I had to do it
I jumped at the chance
A puzzling story
It was dark when I awoke, screaming

2 *Yellow Bird* is told through the eyes of someone looking back to the time when he was nine years old. Rewrite the story from the point of view of his mother or his brother or Mrs Mallion.

3 When Mrs Mallion says of her husband: 'Bill's pushin' up th'daisies' she means he is dead. We sometimes use roundabout expressions to cover up something unpleasant. Such expressions are called euphemisms and there are many concerned with death: 'passed away', 'gone to the eternal sleep', 'with Jesus'. Can you think of any more?

4 The boy in this story has two dreadful nightmares. Sometimes

our dreams seem more real than life itself. Write about a vivid dream you have had. How much do you feel it was influenced by your experiences during the day?

5   Continue the story from where it ends. After you have finished, each of you could read your endings to the rest of the class.

Act it out

1   Find a poem or extract written in a particular dialect and prepare a reading of it.

2   In pairs, act out one of the following scenes:

At Mr Simpson's shop when Jimmy buys the new canary

The conversation between the boy's parents after they have put him to bed

The meeting between Jimmy's mother and Mrs Mallion at the bus stop when the old lady is told what has happened

Geoff's account of the incident when he meets his friend at school the next day.

Further reading

Many writers tell us about when they were children. You might like to read and compare *Yellow Bird* with some other lively accounts of childhood such as: *Quite Early One Morning* by Dylan Thomas, *One Small Boy* and *The Goalkeeper's Revenge* by Bill Naughton, *Harold and Bella, Jammy and Me* by Robert Leeson and *Skulker Wheat* by John Griffin.

The Firework Display

by George Layton

About the story

Have you ever had one of those days when everything seems to go wrong? The writer of this vivid and amusing story recalls just such a time when he was a boy and the old rhyme 'Remember, remember, the fifth of November!' had a particular significance for him.

Talk it over

1 Writers choose the titles for their stories with great care. How does this meaning of *The Firework Display* become fuller after we have read the story?

2 'Why was my mum so difficult? Why did she have to be so old-fashioned?' Parents often have very different ideas from their children about such things as:

   amount of pocket money
   suitable television programmes
   time to go to bed
   friends
   clothes

   What do you disagree with your parents about? Do you try and persuade your mother by telling her, like George, that 'All the other lads at school are ...' or arguing that 'It's not fair!'? How successful are you at making her change her mind?

3 In the collection from which *The Firework Display* is taken, there is a series of photographs, illustrating the various stories. If you were given the job of taking photographs, what parts of the story would you illustrate? What would your photographs feature?

4 *The Firework Display* and *The Ceremony* are similar in a number of ways. Discuss in pairs or in a small group.

5 If you were given the opportunity of meeting George Layton, what questions would you ask him about this story?

Write it down

1 Write about an occasion when you, like George, have been in real trouble at home with your mother or father. Make it as interesting and detailed as you can and try to remember what you and your parents said.

2 When we describe a person we often describe him or her by a short sentence, such as 'He's got a nasty temper' or 'She's always smiling'. Describe in one sentence for each:

George (the boy who is telling the story)
Barry
Norbert
George's mother

3 The day after the disastrous firework display, George starts to write in his diary 'Yesterday, my mum nearly murdered me'. Finish the entry.

4 Continue the story, describing what George's mother said.

5 Read the beginning of the following account by Tessa Quinn called *The Day When Everything Went Wrong*:

It started at eight o'clock! I woke up, stretched, yawned and snuggled back down into the warm bedclothes.

'Tess!' My mum shouted from downstairs. 'Tess, are you going to get up? It's past eight o'clock.'

'Just a few more minutes,' I thought. It was so warm and cosy. When I looked at the clock again it had gone half past eight. I leapt out of bed as if I had been stung on the bottom by a bee and landed on the metal buckle of my satchel.

'Aaaaahhh!' I screamed.

'Stop messing about!' Dad shouted up the stairs, 'And get dressed'. I rushed into the bathroom and squeezed the toothpaste tube madly. A long white, striped worm of toothpaste dropped on the carpet.

'Oh no! Mum!'

'Will you hurry up!' Mum shouted up the stairs.

After a quick wash (I missed the teeth) I went in search

of my school clothes. Of course they were nowhere to be found.

'Mum, where's my clothes?'

'Tess!' mum shrieked. 'Will you hurry up!'

I threw on some clothes and rushed downstairs. I didn't see Jamie's plastic car until I trod on it, slipped and fell headlong down the stairs.

'Aaaahhhh!'

And that was only the start!

Write your own amusing account with the same title.

Act it out

1 Working in pairs, act out one of the following conversations which might have taken place later that evening between

George and his mother
George's mother and his Auntie Doreen
Barry and Norbert
Trevor and his mother/father.

2 It is several years later and George has a family of his own. He tells the story of the disastrous events to his children. Act out the scene.

3 Turn one of the following incidents which appear in this story into a short play:

the scene in the park at the beginning
George tries to persuade his mum to buy some fireworks
George trades his bike for the bag of fireworks
the firework display at the end.

•The following suggestions may be helpful:

•Re-read the story carefully.

•Pick out the scene you wish to dramatise.

•Give yourself a wide margin of about one third of the width of the paper. This will be for speakers' names and any rough production notes.

•Everything which is not spoken should be underlined.

•Write speakers' names in capital letters. You do not need

speech marks.

•The speakers' feelings, reactions, tones of voice should be put into brackets.

Here is the beginning of one dramatisation written by Michael Timmings:

*(George's mum
is busy ironing.
He hovers
nervously
around the
ironing board
and then decides
to ask her).*

GEORGE: Mum.

MUM: Yes?

GEORGE: Can I have some fireworks this year?

MUM: No.

GEORGE: Go on mum.

MUM: I said no!

GEORGE: But why mum? All the other lads at school are having their own fireworks, all of 'em. Why can't I?

*(Mum
carries on
ironing)*

GEORGE: Go on. Mum ...

MUM
*(ignoring
him)*:   It washes well this shirt.

When your script is completed select a producer, nominate a pupil to be in charge of sound effects, and give out the acting parts. After a few rehearsals you will be ready to record your play or present it to the rest of your class.

Further reading

Look out for George Layton on the television and in films at the cinema. He is a well-known actor in addition to being a popular writer. *The Firework Display* comes from a collection of very funny and realistic stories which are based on the author's own childhood experiences in Bradford, West Yorkshire, where he grew up. If you want to find out more about young George, Barry, Trevor and Norbert and hear about other hilarious and often disastrous adventures, then read *A Northern Childhood* by George Layton.

She Was Afraid of Upstairs

by Joan Aiken

About the story

There is a real sense of sadness in this strange, supernatural story about little Tessie who is afraid of going upstairs.

Talk it over

1 Tessie's terror at going upstairs is described as being a phobia, that is, an abnormal fear. There are many, many phobias: hydrophobia is a fear of water, claustrophobia of small spaces, pyrophobia of fire and xenophobia a fear of foreigners. Do you know the names of any more phobias? Are you really frightened by something?

2 Discuss the reaction of Tessie's parents to their daughter's great fear of going upstairs. Does their treatment of her change over the years? What are other people's suggestions for dealing with Tessie? How does Grandfather Moon treat her?

3 Think about the last occasion your parents were angry with you and tried to make you do something you didn't want to do. What were your inner thoughts and feelings at the time? What did you actually do and say?

4 Find the following phrases in the short story and explain what they mean:

'dashing down again as if the Militia were after her'
'Tessie had the diptheery'
'off he goes, in high dudgeon'
'white as a dishclout'.

5 Did you expect the story to end as it did? What do you think the author wanted us to think about by ending the story in this way? Can you think of an alternative ending?

Write it down

1 What sort of atmosphere is created at the beginning which is important for the whole story? After reading the first paragraph

what did you expect this story to be about? Contrast the opening with the ending.

2 What kind of man is Grandfather Moon? Describe him and his way of life.

3 Imagine that you are a reporter for a local newspaper. Write an article describing the strange events at Darkwood Farm. Make the headlines as eye-catching as possible.

4 Write the conversation that might have taken place the next morning between Tessie's parents and Grandfather Moon.

5 Several years later, Aunt Sarah relates the story of little Tessie to her grand-niece or grand-nephew. Write the story.

Act it out

1 'He must have told another doctor about Tessie's wilfulness.' Act out the conversation Tessie's doctor has with the psychologist, Dr Trossick.

2 Uncle Fred and Mr Whitelaw set off to fetch the doctor. Act out their conversation, in which Tessie's father describes his daughter's illness. You might like to include the scene where they arrive at Dr Hastie's house.

3 In groups of four or five, make up a short play about a boy or a girl who is afraid of something.

Further reading

When you start to read a Joan Aiken story you just cannot put it down. She writes beautiful, haunting stories about princes and princesses, mysterious magical stories of other worlds and stories which leave you with a strange tingling feeling. Two short story collections you might like to read are: *The Kingdom Under the Sea* and *A Necklace of Raindrops*. Other books by Joan Aiken include: *The Whispering Mountain*, *The Shadow Guests* and *A Bundle of Nerves*.

The Turning Tide

by David Harmer

About the story

We all remember the fun we had at the seaside, on the sand and in the sea. The school trip to Sandthorpe for pupils of York Street School, however, turns out to be far from funny!

Talk it over

1 How does David Harmer create the tension and build up the anticipation? At what part in the story did you guess that the children might be cut off by the sea?

2 How do your own experiences of school trips compare with those in *The Turning Tide*?

3 The writer implies that Mr Armstrong is not a very good teacher. What parts of the story support this view? What, in your opinion, are the qualities of a 'good' teacher?

Write it down

1 Re-write the story as if one of the following characters is telling it:

Mrs Campbell
Mr Armstrong
Mr Khan
Mrs Rogers
a pupil

2 What is your reaction to the way the story ends? Make up an alternative ending.

3 Write character descriptions of the two teachers who feature in the story. Make a list of words which describe their appearance, thoughts and actions. Look closely at the text to help you build up your pictures.

4 Write a short story called *The School Trip*.

5 Mr Armstrong does not appear to have learned from the near

disaster on the beach. What things should teachers be aware of when taking pupils on school trips? Write a list of 'dos and don'ts'.

6 David Harmer delights in using vivid word pictures, colourful phrases, metaphors and similes. Here are just a few he uses:

'icy rain rattled against her cagoule'
'thin white legs gleaming through the waves'
'like a small, blue, bad-tempered airship'
'a watery sun wobbled out from behind a thick sludge of cloud'

Find more and make a note of them under these headings:
(a) Those I like
(b) Those I do not like

Explain why certain descriptions and details appeal to you and others do not.

Act it out

1 Prepare a dramatic reading of part of the story.

2 When Mr Khan and Javed arrive home that evening, they relate the events of the day to the rest of the family. Act out the scene.

3 Mrs Rogers arrives at school the next day to complain about Mr Armstrong's irresponsible behaviour on the trip to Sandthorpe. Act out the scene where the Headteacher sends for the two teachers to explain what happened.

Further reading

David Harmer teaches in a school in South Yorkshire and has written poems for adults and children. Five of the numerous short stories he has written appear in the collection *Overstone*, published by Arnold-Wheaton. He is presently working on a novel for young people and editing a collection of short stories for schools. He is a member of a dynamic comedy team called The Circus of Poets, a four-part rhythm and rhyme group which tours schools and colleges.

Butch!

by Christine Bentley

About the story

Christine is pleased and excited when she hears great-uncle Alex has left her something in his will. But when that something turns out to be an ugly and unusually bad-tempered dog, she wishes he had not bothered.

Talk it over

1 Christine Bentley based her story on a true incident but, like many writers, she built up the story with details, dialogue and exaggerations. Often truth is stranger that fiction. Can you recall any amusing or memorable stories or incidents which sound far-fetched but which actually happened?

2 Discuss other appropriate titles for this story.

3 What is your reaction to the way the story ends? How did you expect the story to finish?

4 How would you describe this story: as sad, or cruel, or amusing, or silly?

Write it down

1 'When Dad brought it home, I couldn't believe it! I just couldn't believe it!' Use this opening sentence for a story of your own.

2 Write a story telling of the further adventures of Butch.

3 Christine decides to write to Mr Fox explaining what happened. Write the letter.

4 Write a short play in which the central character is an animal.

5 Imagine you are a reporter from a local newspaper assigned to write a feature entitled 'Popular Pets'. Write the article, including details of the interviews with Butch's owners and their neighbours.

Act it out

1 Working in pairs, act out one of the following conversations

which might have taken place between

Christine's father and Uncle Alex's neighbour the day Butch is collected;
Christine and Gillian regarding the arrival of the dog;
the milkman and the postman regarding Butch;
Tracey's father and mother later that day;

2 The local Residents' Association meets to discuss 'the vicious dog' at number 89. Improvise the scene.

Further reading
If you enjoyed this story you might like to read others about unusual and amusing pets: *Skipper and Sam* by Carolyn Dinan, *Mummy's Boy* by Gervase Phinn (Thomas Nelson), *The Midnight Fox* by Betsy Byars (Puffin) and *Dog Days and Cat Naps* by Gene Kemp (Puffin).

Just like Nat Gonella

by Roger Burford-Mason

About the story

'I wanted it so badly,' says the boy in this story. His longing for the trumpet in the junk shop window makes him do something he later regrets.

Talk about it

1 Roger Burford-Mason uses certain significant details to tell us about the boy. For example he says that he wears 'a clean but frayed shirt' and a 'threadbare jacket'. Look through the story and find other clues which help us build up a picture of the boy, his interests and background.

2 What are Mr Sapper's first impressions of the boy?

   Why and how does his attitude change as he gets to know him?
   Why does he 'feel sorry for the lad'?
   Do you think the shopkeeper was too trusting?
   When he discovers that the trumpet is missing, does Mr Sapper deal with the boy too leniently?

3 What does the writer mean when he says:

   'flustered by the boy's silence'
   'made a mental resolution'
   'You could have knocked Sapper over with the proverbial'
   'Finding things gradually became less a voyage of discovery and more a matter of logic.'

4 What is your reaction to the way the story ends?

5 Has *Just Like Nat Gonella* any similarities with other stories in this collection?

Write it down

1 Write a description of Mr Sapper's junk shop. Like the writer of this short story, include details and colourful phrases to create a vivid picture.

2 The boy tells the old shopkeeper that the music lessons are 'the only thing about school I do like'. Imagine you are the boy in the story and write down what you think about school and the other pupils in your class.

3 Continue the story. You might describe the evening of the school concert, to which Mr Sapper is invited, when the boy plays the trumpet and introduces the old man to his parents.

4 Write a short story or play in which you buy something from a junk shop. The object might have magical powers, or be worth a fortune, or be the clue to some mystery.

5 The boy in this story has a paper round. What are the advantages and disadvantages of having a part-time job?

Act it out

1 'Wednesday was a good day for Mr Sapper. He sold four chairs to an American officer and some bric-a-brac to a very airy fairy couple.' Act out a play set in the junk shop in which various people call to buy things. You might include an awkward or angry customer.

2 The boy has to share the trumpet he uses for lessons at school with another pupil who 'never cleans it properly after he's had his go on it'. Act out the argument which the two boys have over the use of the school trumpet.

3 When the boy arrives home with the trumpet he has taken from the junk shop his parents are curious about where he has got it from. Act out the scene.

Further reading

Roger Burford-Mason has written a lot of stories and plays about young people. You may have heard some of them which have been broadcast on BBC schools radio. His play *Schoolboy Snooker Star* was recently published by Longman and another of his plays *Keep on Running* appears in the collection *Stage Write* published by Unwin-Hyman. You can tell from this story that Roger Burford-Mason is a keen jazz musician.

The Great Leapfrog Contest

by William Saroyan

About the story

'Sugar and spice and all things nice ... that's what little girls are made of.' So goes the old nursery rhyme. But Rosie Mahoney, the subject of this short story, is far from this. She is clever and tough, fights the boys and most times wins and she is better than any of them at football, baseball and hockey. All this is too much for the new leader of the gang who decides to show everybody that he, for one, is not going to be beaten by a girl.

Talk it over

1 What clues in the writing tell the reader that this story is set in America?

2 What do you know about Rosie's family? Is the way she behaves in part a result of her background?

3 Why do you think Rex felt 'he ought to prove his superiority'? How would the boys in your class feel about a girl like Rosie? Would the girls feel any differently?

4 How was Rosie 'crafty and shrewd' in the way she played the leapfrog game?

5 Losing the contest 'made a better man of Rex'. Do you agree?

Write it down

1 Here is report slip for Rosie's school:

Subject	Teacher's comments
English	
Maths	
Science	
P.E.	
Geography	
History	

Using the information about her given in the story, write reports for several of the subjects Rosie takes.

2 Rewrite the ending of the story, imagining that either Rosie or Rex is telling it.

3 Write another adventure in the life of Rosie, the 'tough little Irish kid'.

4 The story tells us that Rosie later gave up tomboy activities, became one of the most beautiful girls in town and married one of the wealthiest young men in King's County. Do you think Rosie would have changed so completely as she grew up? How would she now see her childhood? Imagine that you are Rosie and write about your memories.

Or: Write a story about the next five years in Rex's life. Does he too become rich and successful? Does he meet Rosie again?

5 Write your own poem, story or short play about a contest.

Act it out

1 Rosie's teacher asks to see Mr and Mrs Mahoney about their daughter's 'unacceptable behaviour' at school. Act out the interview.

2 When Rex arrives home after the contest he is bruised, dazed and confused. His angry father decides to call and see the parents of 'the little ruffian' who has done this to his son. Act out the scene where Mr Folger visits the Mahoney house.

3 At home that evening Mr and Mrs Mahoney are describing to the rest of the family how difficult and 'tomboyish' their youngest daughter is when Rosie enters - very tired, dusty and sore. Act out the scene.

Further reading

William Saroyan is a man of many parts: author, playwright and song writer amongst other things. One of his plays, *The Time of Your Life*, won the prestigious Pulitzer Prize and in the 1960s the record *Come On-a My House* which he composed sold millions of copies. William Saroyan's son, Aram, was the inspiration for his warm and sensitive novel *My Son Aram* about another 'ordinary kind of kid.' You might like to read it.

Owls are Night Birds

by Berlie Doherty

About the story

Children often get along better with old people than they do with those of their parents' generation. Perhaps it is because old people have the time to listen, or are more easy going, or are not as critical as parents and teachers. In this marvellously warm and sensitively written story about the relationship of a young boy and an old man the themes of loneliness, friendship and even prejudice are explored.

Talk it over

1 What kind of man was Mr Dyson? Describe him and discuss how his way of life changes when Steven begins to visit him.

2 The people in this story give away clues about themselves and about the other characters. Which words do you think would best describe Steven, Elaine and Mrs Dyson?

3 What is it about Mr Dyson and his shop that Elaine dislikes so much?

4 Why is the owl so important in this story?

5 Discuss how Elaine treats her brother. How do you get along with your brother or sister? Are there certain things that you always seem to argue or disagree about?

Write it down

1 Write a poem, description or short passage on how you see yourself when you are old. What do you think you will look like? How will you behave? What will be your interests?

2 Imagine that you are Mr Dyson and that you keep a diary. Write some of the entries, the last being the one before you set out to look for the owl.

3 Working in small groups, devise a colourful and lively booklet called 'Adopt a Granny.' Think carefully about the cover. It needs

to be bright and attractive. Discuss the possible contents. They need to be helpful and clear.

Act it out

1 Working in groups of four, decide which are the most important moments or key incidents in the story. Then create a tableau or still picture showing what is happening.

2 Make up a small play in which Elaine and Steven are interviewed by a newspaper reporter who is interested in writing an article about the albino owl.

3 The children visit Mr Dyson's shop some weeks later. Act out the scene.

Further reading

Berlie Doherty is one of this country's most popular children's writers. Many of her stories, like this one, have been broadcast on radio and two of her children's novels have been dramatised for television. Her stories, which are well worth reading, include *The Making of Fingers Finnigan, Children of Winter, White Peak Farm, How Green You Are, Tough Luck* and *Granny is a Buffer Girl.*

Further ideas

1 Many writers base their stories on something that they have seen or experienced themselves. Which stories in this collection seem to you to be autobiographical? What clues help you to decide?

2 What are the ingredients of a 'good' short story? Discuss your ideas in groups and make a list. Which story did you enjoy the most and which the least? Give reasons.

4 As well as telling an interesting story, writers very often want us to think carefully about a certain theme or issue. Which of the stories in this collection look at similar themes? Have any of the stories made you rethink your opinions or change your views about an issue?

5 Something which you find funny may not amuse another person. There are many forms of humour: slapstick, sick jokes, verbal comedy, situation comedy and a whole lot more. What makes you laugh? Which of these stories did you find the most amusing?

6 Some of the stories are told in the 'first person', that is when the writer tells the story as if it is happening to her or him. Christine Bentley writes in the first person in her story. She says: 'I had always wanted a dog.' Some writers such as Roger Burford-Mason prefer to use the 'third person', when the events concern someone else and he writes: 'Wednesday he had a good day'. What is gained by telling the story in the first person?

7 All the stories in this collection have a strong central character. Which character did you enjoy reading about the most? Did you identify with any of the characters? Write your own story centring on one of these characters.

8 Compare the openings of the various stories. Which were the most promising? Compare the endings; which were the most surprising?

Acknowledgements

The authors and publishers are grateful for permission to reproduce copyright material:

David Harmer for 'The Turning Tide' © 1989; Laurence Pollinger Ltd for 'A Present from the Hartz Mountains' © Gene Kemp; Christine Bentley for 'Butch'; Collins Publishers for 'The Ceremony' from *The Ceromony and other Stories* © Martyn Copus; Methuen Children's Books for 'She was Afraid of Upstairs' © Joan Aiken from *The Methuen Book of Strange Tales*; Longman Group UK for 'The Firework Display' from *A Northern Childhood* by George Layton; Roger Burford-Mason for 'Just Like Nat Gonella'; Bertie Doherty for 'Owls are Night Birds'; Laurence Pollinger Ltd for 'The Great Leapfrog Contest' from *Best Stories of William Saroyan* © William Saroyan; John Latham for 'Yellow Bird'.

We are unable to trace the copyright holders of 'A Mother in Mannville' by Marjorie Kinnan Rawlings and would appreciate any information which would help us do so.

Collections

This new series of anthologies provides you with a fresh and varied collection of material for your 11-14 year old students. **Collections** contains imaginative follow-on activities designed to meet the needs of the National Curriculum. The activities are written to encourage pupils to respond to the material and develop the National Curriculum requirements of reading, writing, listening and speaking. The follow-on material offers individual, pair and group work.

All the ideas prepare students for the GCSE form of study but will also fit in with the Primary and Middle school philosophy of *"first hand experience"*.

Lizard over Ice

A Poetry Anthology

Gervase Phinn

Lizard over Ice is a selection of poetry including: miniatures, haiku, chants, acrostics, shape poems, riddles and many more.

- The poems are modern and traditional, published and unpublished. The selection includes such poets as DH Lawrence, Judith Nicholls, Wes Magee, Philip Larkin, Edward Lear, John Mole, Roy Fuller, Grace Nicholls and many more.

- The sections, based on a form or type of poetry, have a brief introduction and fine examples of poems written by students.

- In compiling the new anthology, Gervase Phinn encourages students to enjoy reading and writing poetry.

- The anthology offers a rich selection of poetry from around the world.

0-17-439211-7

216 x 160mm,   128 pages

Collections 3

A Drama Collection

David Eccles

A new and exciting collection of plays for the lower school. The selection includes drama by well known writers and a specially commissioned play by the children's author, David Williams. The selection is designed to build on current good practice and offers both the experienced teacher and non-specialist stimulating and lively material that allows them to work confidently within the requirements of the National Curiculum and create new and meaningful opportunities for their students.

Each play is supported by follow-on activities which encourage your students to talk about, act out and write about the plays.

0-17-432329-8

216 x 138mm,   144 pages